You'll Understand When You're Dead

MICHELE BARDSLEY

DEDICATION

To my Viking
I love you forever.

To my BFF Renee
You're the reason this book is finished
Love ya!.

CONTENTS

ACKNOWLEDGMENTS

The fans of the Broken Heart series has driven its success from the beginning. Writing about Broken Heart and its residents is such fun for me. I'm so glad you are all part of my world!

"We know a little about a lot of things; just enough to make us dangerous."
~Dean Winchester, *Supernatural*

PROLOGUE

"YOUR MOTHER IS going to kill us," whispered Jenny Matthews. "If my parents find out, they'll kill me, too."

"This from the girl who hid a zombie in a tree house?" Kimberly Haltom punched her best friend in the shoulder.

"Larry isn't a zombie anymore."

"Details!" Kimmie waved off her friend's concerns. "And, we're not going to get into trouble." She dragged Jenny up the porch stairs and to the front door of the two-story house.

Tilda had recently moved to Broken Heart, Oklahoma and had become the ward of the Stinson sisters, who ran the Three Sisters Bed & Breakfast. She had fascinated Kimmie right away with her goth appearance and her mature sophistication.

"What did you tell Tilda?" asked Jenny nervously.

"That my mom needs a push in the right direction. She's lonely. She needs a man."

"I thought you were a feminist."

"I am. Except when it comes to my mom. Let's go."

"Look, I know Tilda's related to the witch sisters. But she's our age. What do you think she's going to do?"

"Something awesome."

THEY SAT IN Tilda's room, an ode to black, and as the teen put it, the "dark forces." Kimmie thought that sounded exciting, but Jenny was more skeptical.

"You don't call up demons, do you?"

"I don't mess with Satan's minions," said Tilda, her kohled eyes wide and her voice a dramatic whisper. "My powers are derived from what dwells in nature."

Jenny rolled her eyes. "Whatever."

Jenny had been raised with paranormals since she was nine, so it was hard to impress her. Kimmie had only been a vampire's daughter for three years, ever since her mom, Natalie Haltom, came home dead. Kimmie had been born and raised in Las Vegas, Nevada. Her parents divorced when she was thirteen. As if that hadn't been traumatic enough, three months later her mom became a bloodsucker.

She didn't really know how it happened.

One night, she was rousted out of bed by a paranormal private detective named Ash, with her weird eyes and spiky hair and scowling expression, and told to pack one bag. Kimmie later learned that Ash had rescued her mother from some kind of vampire gang, or whatever, and had called in Queen Patsy to vampify her. It was that or death, and Kimmie had been all for the vampire thing. Living without her mother was not something she could think about, especially after the way her dad had abandoned them.

Anyway.

She and Mom moved to Broken Heart, where vampires could actually eat real food—because of some pixie spell or whatever—and her mother, who'd been a caterer in her old life, had gotten a new start as a vampire baker.

Mom didn't date, spending all her time either baking new confections with names like Bloody Good Cupcakes (this was like a lava cake except thickened blood oozed out instead of chocolate) and Wolf 'Em Down Delights, which the werewolves loved. Because dogs, whether domestic or wild or shifter, wanted treats.

"Did you bring what I asked?" Tilda's big eyes stared at Kimmie unblinkingly.

"Yeah." She opened her purse and took out the blue silk bra. "You sure this is gonna work?"

"If we want to draw men to your mother's life, we must start with the basics."

"So you're going to put the juju on her bra?" asked Jenny.

Tilda spared Jenny a haughty look. "Spells require direction."

"Then I guess it's good we're directing 'em right at Mrs. Haltom's boobs."

"Jenny," hissed Kimmie, "shut up."

Jenny pressed her lips together.

Tilda put the bra in the middle of a white circle

she'd drawn on the wood flooring. Votive candles, in a range of colors and scents, ringed the outside. She sat down and held out her hands. Jenny sat to her left, Kimmie to the right, and they joined hands.

Tilda took a deep breath and said, "Let us begin."

For a moment, all they heard was the snap of the tiny flames and the melodramatic heaving breaths of Tilda. Excitement fluttered in Kimmie's belly. She had to believe she was doing what was best for her mom.

"I am now in tune with the spirits and the dark elements of nature," intoned Tilda. "Tell them what you want."

"I need my hand back," said Kimmie.

Tilda popped open one eye. "You can't break the circle."

"But I wrote it all down. I don't have it memorized."

Tilda sighed. "Fine. But don't take too long. The broken circle offers a portal to the other side, and we don't want spirits coming through."

Kimmie let go of Jenny's hand and dug around in her front jean pocket. She pulled out a torn piece of notebook paper.

"Natalie Haltom is one hot mama who needs excitement in her love life. She's gorgeous and smart and bakes awesome cookies. Respondents should be good-looking, and it helps if they're dead."

"One hot mama? That's lame," said Jenny.

"She's right," said Tilda. "Super lame."

"Besides," said Jenny, "what if you get some toe-sucking perv or a stake wielding Van Helsing wannabe?"

"That's why we're being specific. Hel-*lo*, dead guys

only."

"Why can't we hook up your mom in the normal way?"

"Jenny, we live in Broken Heart, the capital of weird. There is no normal here. Besides, anyone mom sleeps with, she'll be tied to for a hundred years, so he has to be a nice, decent guy."

Tilda raised a thin-plucked brow drawing attention to her silver eyebrow ring. "Are you finished with your request?"

"Yeah. I guess so." Kimmie shoved the paper back into her pocket, hoping she got it right, and took Jenny's hand again.

"We ask the spirits to grant the request of this vampire's daughter so that her mother might find eternal love. Or at least, love for the next century." Tilda exhaled, rolled her eyes back in a dramatic display, and intoned, "We now close the circle to the otherworld and thank the spirits for their help."

Tilda opened her eyes and let go of Kimmie and Jenny's hands. "Help me blow out the candles. My aunts will freak if they know I'm casting."

Jenny shook her head. "This is not going to end well."

Kimmie hoped her friend was wrong.

CHAPTER ONE

"EXCUSE ME."

Matthew Dennison looked around, but only saw the green field stretching before him. Other than him, the only other occupant in the field was a cow—albeit a dead one. He idly wondered why there was a ghost cow trying to munch on the dew-laden grass. Though he'd only lived here a couple of weeks, he found that in Broken Heart, Oklahoma, they freshly stocked the crazy every day. The neighborhood where he'd settled was nestled at the bottom of the hill behind the oak tree. He'd gotten into the habit of walking up to this parcel of farmland to enjoy the first part of the evening. The crickets chirped merrily.

Matt inhaled the sweet scent of honeysuckle and fresh air as he readjusted his position under the huge century-old oak tree. His rear end tingled from sitting on the rocky ground. Stars dotted the night sky, and he'd spent a pleasant few minutes simply staring at the beautiful sky above him. The wind ruffled his too long hair, and he pushed it back.

"Seriously. Are you ignoring me?"

Well, it wasn't the dead cow talking. Maybe it was another spirit—one that sounded distinctly like an irritated female.

"I don't see you," he said.

"Try looking up."

Matt did as directed, his gaze searching the thick branches of the oak. He spotted a very much alive woman clinging to the massive trunk. She was dressed in a pink T-shirt, whitewashed jeans, and sneakers. Her silky chestnut locks were pulled into a ponytail. Defiant brown eyes dared him to ask why she was stuck in a tree.

He liked a good dare. "Why are you in a tree?"

"I'm hiding from the cow."

Matt jerked a thumb over his shoulder. "You mean the dead one?"

"You can see ghosts?" she asked. "I thought that was only a Family Amahté ability. And I know you're not a vampire."

"I'm a psychic." A powerful one. Formerly of the Vedere clan, Matt had walked away from the only family he'd ever known. Discovered at the age of eight in the New York City foster care system by a Vedere psychic, Matt had been whisked away to the group's compound in upper Connecticut.

The woman studied him, and he suddenly felt self-conscious. "I take it you're an Amahté vampire?"

"Yes." She blew out an unnecessary breath, which meant she probably hadn't been a vampire for very long. "There are apple trees on the other side of the

7

field. Since I'm baking pies today, I thought it would be nice to get some fresh apples. Then Hell Cow showed up."

Matt waited for the rest of the story. When she went mute, he asked, "Are you afraid of cows or just cow spirits?"

For a moment, she stared at him, and then she sighed. "My vampire power has a quirk," she said. "Ghosts have physicality for me. They're as real and solid as you are, and that one—" She stabbed finger toward the bovine. "—bit me on the ass, and then chased me up this tree."

Matt looked at the cow. The creature was still munching on grass, although not really, because ghosts didn't need sustenance.

"Jump down," he said. "I'll catch you."

The idea did not thrill her if the expression on her face was any indication. Matt craned his neck. Maybe she was just in pain from a wayward branch poking her backside.

Finally, she said, "All right. I'll jump."

Matt obligingly opened his arms, but she didn't loose her death grip from the limb. In fact, she looked as if she were contemplating staying in the tree. A man of action, he reached up, grabbed her ankle, and yanked. He heard an ominous ripping sound, the scrape of her shoe against the bark, and then a scream worthy of a horror-movie heroine.

She plummeted from the tree. Matt managed to catch her, but he was thrown off-balance and tumbled backwards. As he fell, he wrapped his arms around her and held on tightly to protect her as he smacked into the ground. Matt sucked in a breath. Grass tickled his face. He hoped he hadn't damaged any vital organs. And he certainly hoped the rocks impaling him hadn't punctured his flesh. The woman, whose head had rapped his chin during the fall, lifted up and glared at him.

"Quit copping a feel."

His hands flexed automatically on her nicely rounded jean-clad buttocks. Matt obliged her request. "I'm sorry. I didn't mean to—er, grab you."

"Yes. Well." She rolled off, stumbling to her feet. Matt watched as she smoothed back the sweaty curls loosed from her ponytail and straightened her dirt-splotched shirt and torn jeans.

He got to his feet, dragging in deep breaths, and cursed the ache traveling up his spine. He rubbed a sore spot on his thigh. "My name is Matt Dennison," he said. "Nice to meet you."

Her grim expression eased, and when she unpinched her lips, he was surprised to see she had a nice, full, kissable mouth. She dusted off her hands and offered one to him. Her grip was dainty, feminine, and surprisingly firm. "I'm Natalie Haltom. Thanks for the rescue."

He executed a courtly bow. "I'm glad to be of service."

"I'm glad we didn't end up in the emergency room." She smiled. Wow. She really did have a nice mouth. "I'm giving up on the apples." She eyed the cow at the far end of the field then her gaze flitted over him. "I'll see you around, Matt." She turned around, presumably to go home, but Matt didn't want her to go. Not yet.

"You're going to let the cow win?" he asked.

She faced him again, her expression resolved. "Uh … yeah. Totally."

"I'll get the apples for you."

"It's okay," she said. "I have some fresh strawberries. I'll make tarts."

"I love tarts." Actually, Matt had no idea if he liked them or not because he'd never had one. But he wanted her to stay. It had been a while since he'd dated, and she was the first woman since Vera, his ex and the reason for his recent move to Broken Heart, to engage his interest. Not to mention his hormones. The basic, primal part of him wanted her in bed. Now.

The cow mooed.

He saw Natalie's eyes widen. Then he heard clomping sounds. He looked over his shoulder and saw the cow running toward them, head down.

Natalie yelped, and whirled around, running toward the neighborhood where he lived. The cow galloped around him, but as it passed the oak tree, it turned misty and then disappeared all together.

"Natalie!"

"Later," she screamed.

Okay, then. He watched Natalie clear the wooden fence that blocked off this land from the neighborhood and head down Brooker Street. Broken Heart was a small community. Exactly the kind of place he'd wanted to start a new life. And it appeared that the charming vampire Natalie lived one street over from him.

After she went into a one-story Ranch house painted a light green, Matt looked up to the sky. The stars winked at him, and he smiled.

NATALIE TOOK A quick shower and changed into a new pair of jeans and a T-shirt that said, "Bakers

Dough It Better." She eschewed shoes and padded into the kitchen, the tiled floor cool on her bare feet. When she'd died, thanks to her ex-husband and his boss AKA cult leader, her last thoughts had been about her daughter Kimmie.

And also killing her ex-husband.

Because, really, what an asshole.

As she started putting together items to make strawberry tarts—maybe with some O blood sauce drizzled on top, her mind wandered to the hot psychic with muscles like steel. He was eight kinds of yummy. It'd been ages since a man had touched her anywhere, much less her rear end. Her butt had tingled all the way home.

New people—and she used that term lightly— moved into Broken Heart all the time. It was a thriving community of paranormals that included vampires, werewolves, werecats, fairies, zombies, and, apparently, psychics.

The Vederes were a big deal, at least for the paranormal powers-that-be, because they saw the future and created prophecies. She supposed they did other things, too, but nothing that trickled down to the middle-class vampire. Her death had been about baking and parenting.

The doorbell rang.

Crap. She could only think of two people who might visit her at this time of night—her neighbors, the Smiths. They were nice people, or rather nice fae, and she generally enjoyed their company. They were old—like a couple thousand years old—but they only looked like a couple in their early seventies. Bettie Smith loved gossip more than anything, and Natalie could only hope Bettie hadn't seen her running down the street like a full-on idiot. If she had, the entire town would hear about it, only by the time Bettie was done embellishing, Natalie would be naked or on fire or both.

Natalie scuffled to the door and peered through the peephole. Red roses blocked the view. Wait. Roses?

"Who is it?" she asked.

"It's me, pumpkin. Your true love." The voice was male, unfamiliar, and coming from someone hidden behind the flowers.

"You have the wrong house."

"This is Natalie Haltom's home, is it not?"

"Yes."

"These are for you, my adored one."

She slid the chain lock into place and opened the door. "Who are you?"

"Jerry Freid," he said. "I'm answering your call, honeybuns."

"I didn't call anyone."

The roses parted to reveal a dough-faced, balding man whose height left him breast level to her. "Can I come in?"

He was a ghost. The only difference between people and spirits who lived on the earthly plane was that the ghosts had a soft white glow around them. Otherwise, with her ability to physically touch spirits, she would have a hard time figuring out who was alive, dead, or undead.

"I know a good afterlife counselor," she said.

"I'm here for you," he said. His expression had turned stubborn. "You didn't already pick someone, did you?"

"Pick someone for what?"

"For love." He peered around her. "Will you let me in?"

"No." Inviting ghosts into your home made it especially difficult to get them out. They were territorial, and one temper tantrum from a spirit could level an entire room in five minutes. So, no, Jerry was not coming into her home. She undid the chain and stepped onto the porch, shutting the door firmly behind her.

"Look, Jerry," she said gently, "I don't know why you're here. I didn't call you. But if you need help, I can refer you to someone. Someone who isn't me."

"Am I interrupting?"

Natalie looked across Jerry's shiny head at Matt Dennison. He was bare-chested for some reason. She couldn't stop her gaze from gliding over his pectorals to his abs, all tight hard muscle. Her mouth went dry. Then she noticed the T-shirt he held in front of him filled with apples.

"You got those for me?"

"If the lady wants apples for pie, then apples for pie the lady shall get."

"Who is he?" demanded Jerry. He pinned Natalie with an accusing stare. "You said dead people. He shouldn't be in the running, because he's obviously still breathing." A diamond the size of a marble appeared among the roses. "I was here first! So marry me."

Natalie blinked down at the ghost. "I just met you five minutes ago," she said.

"We'll have centuries to get to know each other. Well, you know, after you die." He peered at her. "When do you think that'll happen?"

"Never," she said. "I'm already undead."

He sighed. The roses in his hand wilted, and then faded away. The engagement ring disappeared, too. "I came on too strong, didn't I?"

He was too pathetic to be a serial killer or even a really effective stalker. She sorta felt bad for him, because he was dead and being a spirit was no picnic. Still. Why in the hell did he believe she was on the ghost-dating market?

Jerry puffed himself up, straightened eye-bleeding orange tie and faced Natalie. "I'm not a quitter," he said. "That's why I was named Salesman of the Year five years running. I sold insurance, in case you're wondering. But that's not really a skill you need in the afterlife."

Panic rose inside her as she realized Jerry was not going to go away. If she wanted him gone, he'd have to be exorcised, and she hated doing that because the ghosts were relegated to the world-between-worlds. Limbo.

Shit.

She glanced at Matt and saw his amused expression. *This is so not funny.*

Oh, it's funny.

Natalie blinked. You can hear my thoughts?

I'd be able to hear your thoughts if I was on Mars. You're blasting them like the speakers at a KISS concert.

Get out of my head. She imagined shoving Matt outside a big, metal door and slamming it shut. She felt some satisfaction when she saw him flinch.

"This is a little awkward," said Jerry, in a massive understatement. "Perhaps I could go inside while you tell him off."

"You can't go into my house."

"But you are going to tell him off, right?" asked Jerry, hopefully.

"No, she's not," said Matt. He tied up his T-shirt and placed the apple-laden material onto a nearby table. Then he reached forward and took Natalie's hand, drawing her into his embrace. "You see, Jerry. We're already engaged."

CHAPTER TWO

NATALIE COULDN'T BELIEVE what she'd just heard. Matt looked at her for confirmation, and she realized that it was either a sudden engagement with the psychic or dealing with a wanna-be ghost boyfriend.

"He's definitely my fiancé," she said.

"Yep. Here I am," said Matt. "In the flesh."

Jerry bristled. "Flesh is overrated." He reached and patted Natalie's arm. He looked shocked—and then he patted her again. "I can feel you," he said. He pinched her.

"Ow!"

"You can feel me, too."

He reached for her arm again, and she moved away from him and closer to Matt. "Will you please stop that?"

"It's been so long since I could touch someone—I mean on the earthly plane. In the spirit realm you don't really need human sensory experiences."

"Maybe you should go back to the spirit realm," she said.

"Oh, I can't do that. The door's closed. It was only open crack, mind you, but several us made it through."

Natalie and Matt shared a startled glance, and then stared at Jerry.

"Someone opened a portal in Broken Heart?" asked Matt. "How many spirits escaped?"

Jerry shrugged. "I don't know. It's not like we had a meeting." He looked at Natalie. "You probably shouldn't have asked us for a love life if you already had one."

"You've been busy," Matt whispered into her ear. His warm breath tickled the sensitive skin, and she shivered. Not to mention she was pressed against his muscled form and, for some reason, she felt hot. Liquid. Melting into the heat of Matt. Oh, no. No, no, no. The last time she listened to her va-jay-jay, she ended up dead.

"I didn't put out a call," she finally said.

"Don't deny it. This is preposterous." Jerry pulled down his ill-fitting powder-blue jacket and straightened into a stiff I'm-not-leaving stance. "I don't think you fell in love with this tall hairy—cretin." He nodded sharply at Matt. "That's right. *Cretin.*"

"Did he just call me a cretin?"

"Yes," Natalie said, glancing at Matt's amazed features. "Of the tall, hairy variety."

He frowned, his expression not at all friendly.

What if he didn't take insults well? What if cretin was a rage word—and it turned him into a heaving, maniacal psychic? She wondered if he could blow stuff up with his mind.

Suddenly, Matt leaned down and whispered, "What's a cretin?"

"It's not a compliment, "she whispered back, looking at Jerry. She couldn't help but feel sorry for the infatuated ghost.

Jerry watched Matt stroke her arm, and he turned an alarming shade of red for a creature without a pulse. He heaved a breath, ran a palm over his head, and said, "I'm not giving you up without a fight."

"It appears our ghostly friend needs convincing," Matt said. The rich timbre of his voice had a liquid quality that made her nerves tingle. The lazy intent glittering in his green eyes warned her, but before she could protest, he lowered his head and pressed warm, soft lips against her mouth. Shocked into stillness, she didn't move when Matt pulled her closer and deepened the kiss. He tasted of coffee and mint, and his lips did not demand, but coaxed. She responded far too easily, but it had been a long time since she'd been kissed. And she couldn't remember the experience ever being like this. His tongue flicked the corner of her mouth, and a pure jolt of electricity zapped the pit of her stomach. She pulled back and found herself hanging onto Matt's broad shoulders and gasping for breath.

"Oh dear," Jerry said. His round face deflated like a balloon. "I guess that's it, then."

Jerry's morose features sent pinpricks of guilt through Natalie. Then he offered a beaming smile. His chubby fingers squeezed her arm. "Don't worry, sweetie. I'll be here to pick up the pieces of your heart when this flesh-freak breaks it." Jerry glared at Matt. "Muscles and good looks aren't everything, you know."

Then he shuffled off the porch, down the sidewalk, and faded into mist, drifting away.

"This isn't good," she said. "We need to tell Patsy that there's a lovesick ghost propositioning women."

"I didn't get any bad vibes from him," said Matt. "He's more confused than anything."

Natalie found herself staring at his mouth, and that reminded her that she'd just been the recipient of those fantastic lips.

"You didn't need to kiss me," she said. She really should step away from him. The problem was that her body did not want to listen to her brain, and it didn't help that Muscular Matt seemed content to keep her in his arms.

"All in the line of duty, Natalie."

She pried herself out of his embrace. "I really have no idea what Jerry is talking about, by the way. I didn't send out any kind of invite for some supernatural love life. I'm just fine on my own," she said, not really believing her line about being fine on her own. She looked at his T-shirt full of fruit bounty, then sneaked a glance at his naked, chiseled abs the shirt no longer covered, and back to the apples. Yum. "It was nice of you to get the apples."

"I'm a nice guy."

She wasn't sure how to respond to that, so she said nothing. Instead, she picked up the shirt and said, "Come inside. I'll put the apples in the kitchen and give you back your shirt."

A shame, really. The man should never, ever wear

shirts.

Matt followed her into the house, and she knew his curious gaze was taking in her eclectic knick-knacks, the comfortable furniture, and the walls filled with abstract art.

"What brings you to Broken Heart?" she asked. She untied the shirt and poured the apples into the farmhouse sink. She resisted the urge to toss the shirt into the garbage disposal and hit the switch. Instead, she handed it back to him. "Here you go."

Matt put it on, much to her disappointment, and smiled. "Patsy offered me a job."

"Resident psychic?"

"Something like that."

"Hmm." She put the apples into a colander and rinsed them. "I thought Vedere psychics stayed in their communes."

"Most of them do. One of our younger members was Turned, and she lives here now. We stayed in touch, and when I decided to go my own way, I thought Broken Heart would be a good place to settle. Queen Patsy agreed and ... here I am."

Natalie thought he was giving her a very sanitized version of what had happened, but it wasn't her business anyway. She had her own past with secrets that she preferred no one knew, especially Kimmie. Her daughter didn't know about her dad, the vampire cult, or the fact that he'd sacrificed Natalie to the "Dark One."

His real name had been Phil. But he made his cultists called him Dark One.

Gawd.

"Do you?" Matt asked.

Natalie blinked, jarred out of her thoughts by the

sound of his voice. "Do I what?"

He put his hand on his heart. "Ouch. I asked if you wanted to go out. I mean if we're going to get married, we should probably date first." He grinned.

She couldn't resist grinning back. "You have a point." Then she shook her head. "I don't date. Ever."

"Why?"

Because I was tricked into a blind date with the vampire who killed me. And, oh yeah, my ex-husband set it all up because he's a jerkface. And now that I'm a vampire, there's no such thing as a one-night stand, and I'm not up for another long-term relationship. "It's a long story," she said.

His gaze flicked to her mouth, and she couldn't help but remember that hot kiss he'd planted on her. She had a feeling he wanted to do it again.

So did she. A lot.

"Well, do you suppose I've at least earned a pie?" he asked.

"You jerked me out of a tree, and then let a cow chase me down a hill." She hid her smile. "I hardly think that's pie-worthy behavior."

"I saved you from the ghost."

"Yes. He was terrifying." She put a hand to her chest. "Thanks for your gallant protection," she said drily.

"I could kiss you again."

Natalie turned and looked up at him. "You know the deal with vampires, right? Dating leads to sex, and sex with vampires leads to hundred-year marriages."

"No dating," he said. "Got it. But I can have a pie, right?"

"Yes," she said, relenting. "I will make you an apple pie."

"Thank you." He looked as though he might do something stupid, like kiss her again. "I have to meet Patsy in a few minutes. I'll tell her about Jerry and the portal he mentioned."

"Thanks. Swing by later," she said. "So you can get your dessert."

She wished he was the dessert, but gorgeous men with meltingly good kissing techniques were not on the menu. Too bad because Matt looked yummy, and she bet he tasted yummy, too.

He waved at her. "See you soon, Natalie."

There was a promise in his voice, and she had the feeling he hadn't given up on the dating thing. He left the kitchen, and she heard the front open and shut. She leaned against the kitchen counter, trying to shake off the lust clinging to her like so much powdered sugar.

Yeah. Not happening.

"SORRY ABOUT THE meeting place," said Patsy as Matt sat down next to her on the stone bench. Stretched out before them was the Broken Heart cemetery. "This is the quietest spot in town."

"How are your children?"

"Currently torturing their father."

Matt laughed. His gaze strayed to a nearby tree, and he thought of Natalie. He liked her. He thought she probably liked him too. He'd never dated a vampire before, but Natalie was easy to be around— beautiful, funny, *and* she baked. He was a sucker for dessert.

"Vera called me."

Matt's stomach squeezed. His ex-fiancé was a member of the Supreme Council, one of the top

Vedere psychics who oversaw the American branches of the psychic society. They were the paranormal world's prophets—a heady responsibility. A year ago, Matt had discovered Vera was sleeping with another council member. Her deception unraveled from there. She wasn't in love with Matt. She wanted his power. She wanted to make a play for Vedere leadership—a play that could well fracture the society. She'd been recruiting some of the most talented of the Vedere. Matt wanted no part of her machinations. So, he left. He spent that time traveling, thinking, and finally, deciding what he wanted for his future—a future that did not include the Vera, the Vederes, or issuing prophesies.

"What did she want?" he asked softly.

"She says she has a prophecy for Broken Heart and wants to deliver it in person."

"Don't trust her, Patsy."

"I told her no. The Vedere psychics can suck it as far as I'm concerned." Patsy patted his leg in a motherly fashion. "You're safe here."

"I know."

Patsy's gaze swept over the cemetery, and then her eyes widened. "Is that a cow?"

Matt followed her gaze and saw the ghost cow again. It was munching on the grass near a row of moss-covered tombstones. It lifted its head and mooed.

"Definitely a cow," said Matt. "I saw him earlier in a field outside my neighborhood."

"Animal spirits never linger."

Matt explained what had happened earlier in the evening, from Natalie hiding in the tree to Jerry the Libidinous Ghost. He skipped the part about the fake engagement and the promising kiss that curled his toes.

"A portal. Well, damn."

The cow mooed again and meandered away, drifting into mist.

"We'll have to stay alert about spirit activity," said Patsy. "And find out why a portal opened at all."

"Um … Patsy?"

"Yeah?"

Matt pointed. Dead people were crawling out of the same graves where Ghost Cow had tried to nibble grass. Coincidence?

"It's been a while since we had a zombie outbreak," said Patsy. "I guess I should put 'em back to sleep."

"A vampire queen's work is never done," said Matt.

"True story."

NATALIE SLID INTO the café's bright red booth, ordered a cup of coffee and the biggest piece of peanut butter pie available.

Jessica and Eva looked at her with raised eyebrows.

"It's been that kind of day," she said. "Don't judge."

"Judge? I'm inspired," said Jess. "I want one, too."

"You should probably just bring us the whole pie and three forks," said Eva.

The waitress nodded and left.

Natalie was dying to ask the girls, mated vampires themselves, about dating, love, and the dirt on Matt Dennison. Alas, she had another topic that needed to be discussed first.

"I think Kimmie has a crush."

Eva, who sat next to Natalie, squeezed her shoulder in a show of support. "She's sixteen. I wouldn't be too concerned."

"What if it's someone inappropriate? Like an older guy."

That got their attention.

"Who?" asked Jessica.

"Jason Burnside," said Natalie.

Startled, Eva blurted, "The math teacher?"

"Jason is cute." Natalie accepted a fork from the waitress. As soon as the other two ladies got their utensils, they dug into the gooey goodness. "Well, for someone who's four-hundred-years-old."

"He died at twenty-one, so he looks like a college student. Do you really think Kimmie is enamored of him?" Eva's eyes flashed red. "Did he do something to encourage her?"

Since Eva was the coordinator of education for Broken Heart's children, she took anything to do with the students, school, or teachers very personally.

"I doubt it." Natalie sighed. "She's been experimenting with her identity. Clothes. Make-up. Hairstyles. So why not boys?" She leaned in and whispered, "I found evidence."

"What did you do? Read her diary?" Jessica's eyes widened she finished her first bite. "Wow. This is pretty good for something's that not chocolate."

Natalie squirmed. Her vampire friend's assessment was too close for comfort. "When I was dumping out Kimmie's waste basket, a piece of paper fell out."

She reached into her purse and pulled out a crumpled sheet of notebook paper. She put it on the table.

Eva opened it and smoothed it out. She read, "J is sexy, sweet. A smile with no lips. I like him, but I'm afraid. Math is our common ground. A number plus a number equals infinity. That's how long I'd have to wait for J."

"What makes you think she means Jason?" asked Jessica.

Natalie grasped the paper and turned it over. A scrawled note was on the back. Eva read, "Mr. Burnside is cute, single and dead. Date?"

Then underneath in a different ink and handwriting: "You need therapy."

"Let me see that." Jessica took the note and looked at it for a long moment. "Jenny wrote the therapy part. She writes the letter E all weird. And she's also well known for her sarcasm."

"I wonder where she gets that," said Eva, smiling.

Jessica laughed.

Eva turned to Natalie. "Have you talked with her about this? Asked her what's going on?"

Natalie tucked the paper back into her purse. "No. Kimmie's been trying to rebel, and I'm attempting to support her efforts."

"Teens are strange creatures," said Eva. "One week they're in love, the next they're not. You don't really know if the poem is about Jason." She looked thoughtful. "There are two boys in that class whose names begin with J."

Natalie perked up. "That's great. Maybe she likes one of them. What are their names?"

"There's Jefferson. Well, he goes by his middle name, Hayden. He's intellectual. Nice and quiet. Likes to wear ties to class. Excellent student. His dad is Elliot Wickham—you know, the biologist who works with Stan?"

"Is that the guy who got too many gamma rays and turns green when he gets mad?" asked Jessica.

"No. That's the Hulk. Elliot is a vampire from Iowa."

"Who's the other kid?" asked Natalie.

"He's smart, too. Tall. Enjoys the color black." Eva stared at her pie. "He only has three facial piercings."

Natalie winced.

"His real name is Jeremiah," continued Eva. "But he insists everybody calls him Jackal."

"Jack-hole." Jessica smirked.

Natalie put her fork down ignoring Jess. "Seriously? Jackal?" She wanted to be the buoy in Kimmie's stormy attempts at rebellion. Keeping an open mind, not allowing Kimmie's antics to overwhelm her, and staying away from huge doses of Valium had been part of her crusade to remain a "cool" mother. Letting her only child date a boy named Jackal, though, would be the true test of her motherhood. She sunk lower into the booth. "Oh, give me strength."

"Two more years, and then it's time for college," said Jessica.

"Are those zombies?" Eva stared out the large window of the café.

Natalie looked outside. Five zombies who used to be girls, given the rotted dresses still dangling from their corpses, and five zombie guys, dressed in shredded suits, faced each other on the street.

"Crap. Not again. The last time we had a zombie outbreak, I ended up with spaghetti in my hair." Jessica scooted out of the booth, and Natalie and Eva followed her outside.

To Natalie's amazement, the ghost cow wandered between the zombies, who didn't seem to notice it, and then it disappeared.

Ten zombie screams echoed into the night.

Oh, shit.

CHAPTER THREE

BY THE TIME Patsy and Matt reached downtown, the zombies were in the middle of the street. Patsy nearly curbed the Mercedes as she parked. "They've never ignored my commands before. I'm the fucking queen." She cocked her head. "Is that Abba?"

Matt listened. "Yeah. *Waterloo*, I think."

They were too late.

The zombies had already started their newest brand of terror.

Matt saw Natalie, Eva, and Jessica standing outside the Broken Heart Café. He and Patsy joined them, and they stared at the shambling zombies. The Abba song echoed downtown, courtesy of Jessica's iPhone.

"What the hell are they doing?" groused Patsy.

"I think it's a dance contest," said Jessica. "They were doing it without music, so I thought I'd help." She grinned. "I hope couple number three wins."

Matt watched the zombies dance. Each couple was attempting different moves, but since zombies lacked coordination, they sorta shuffled around each other. One guy's arm fell off, and he picked it up, and held it in the air like a baton. His partner groaned her approval.

"Lord-a-mercy," muttered Patsy. "All right, y'all. Help me corral them back toward the cemetery."

"Aw. Can't we wait to see who wins?" asked Jessica. One glare from Patsy, and she lifted her hands in surrender. "All right. Sheesh." She turned off the music.

SINCE NATALIE WAS Family Amahté, too, she helped Patsy guide and direct the zombies back to the cemetery. They were reluctant to say the least. Finally, though, they returned to their graves, and Patsy was able to command them to "stay there, damn it." Thank goodness for vampire strength. They got the corpses re-buried in no time at all.

When it was all said and done, Natalie was ready to go home and get the cemetery dirt off her shoes.

"I can give you a ride," said Matt.

"My car's downtown," said Natalie.

"Then I'll drop you off there."

"Thanks." With a smile and a wave, she said good-bye to the other vampires, who all piled into Patsy's Mercedes. She saw the looks she got because of Matt and knew the next time she saw her friends, questions would be asked. She got into Matt's black Jeep and strapped in.

The drive to her car only took a few minutes, and they rode in comfortable silence. Matt pulled up behind her minivan.

"Thanks again."

"Any time," said Matt.

"I didn't forget about your pie," said Natalie.

"Neither did I." He grinned.

She wanted to melt against him again and feel his lips on hers. She wanted to be touched and loved and—*whoa*. She reigned in her libido and got out of the car before she did something really stupid. Like shackle a hot stranger to her for a hundred years.

"'Bye, Natalie," he said.

She waved and watched him drive off.

Why did the man have to be so damned appetizing?

MATT SAT CROSS-LEGGED on the reed mat, trying to center his thoughts. Unfortunately, his attempts to calm his chi—not to mention his hormones—were not working. He needed to take an out-of-body trip to Connecticut to see what Vera was plotting. He didn't believe for an instant that she wanted to help Patsy or Broken Heart.

His thoughts drifted to Natalie.

Her bow mouth.

Her sparkling brown eyes.

Her soft skin.

"Fuck." Matt opened his eyes. He needed to detox his mind, but he couldn't with the thoughts of the pretty vampire baker consuming him. Matt rolled to his feet. He might as well raid the refrigerator and catch some television. Ignoring the robe draped over the dresser, he left the bedroom and went into the kitchen. With the AC cranked up, goose pimples rose on his flesh, but he liked it cold in the house, especially since Oklahoma summers were hellishly hot.

Opening the fridge, he peered at the sparse offerings. He needed to go grocery shopping. Tomorrow. He settled for an apple and milk, though as a rule, late night jaunts required junk food, not good-for-you stuff. As he poured the milk, he heard a rustling sound outside the back door.

Stray cats, he thought. He usually put leftovers out for them. He grabbed a bowl of tuna salad from the fridge and sniffed it. The smell didn't make him gag, so he figured it wasn't science experiment material yet. Opening the back door, Matt bent over and placed the bowl on the porch. The bordering bushes on the right shook fiercely.

The foliage parted, and a female figure tumbled backwards and hit the concrete with a thump. A black baseball cap rolled into the yard. Chestnut hair tumbled around the woman's pale face. He leaned closer as a pair of baleful brown eyes glared at him.

"Natalie?"

"I brought your pie," she said.

"Were you hiding it in the bushes?" He looked around. "Where is it?"

"Here you go." She rolled over and Matt saw the remnants of an apple pie. It was flattened against the sidewalk, the crust mere crumbs and the apples nothing but juice.

"I'm gonna cry." If nothing else to keep myself from laughing.

"I'll make you another one," she said. "But you'll have to come to my house to get it."

"Deal." He watched her get onto her hands and knees. Pie decorated her backside like a Pollock painting. "Why don't you come inside and clean up?"

"Yeah." She turned, dusting off her pants, and then straightened. Her mouth dropped open. "Oh. My. God."

Matt whirled around, but the kitchen was empty. Turning back, he stared at Natalie, wondering if she'd hit her head. "What?" he said. "What is it? A spider?" He dusted at his shoulders. "I hate spiders."

"You're naked," she said, her voice going hoarse. "Very, very naked."

Matt looked down. Oh damn. He was naked. He'd forgotten. "I was meditating."

"Oh," Natalie said. "That doesn't explain it at all."

Matt pushed open the door. "Come inside. I'll get dressed, and then I'll help you get the pie off your shirt. Unless, of course, you had other plans for me?" He waggled his brows.

A ghost of a smile flitted across her lips. "Sorry. I only came over to kill your apple pie and make a fool of myself."

"That's what all the girls say."

She laughed. "Okay, Lothario. Go get some clothes on already."

Matt hurried to the bedroom and put on a pair of jean shorts and a tank top. He grabbed an extra T-shirt for Natalie and showed her to the bathroom. When she returned to the kitchen, she wore his gray T-shirt, which hung down to her knees. He liked the way she looked in it.

"You want me to throw that in the washer?"

Natalie glanced down at the bundled shirt in her hands as if she'd just realized she was still holding it. "No, thanks. I appreciate the loaner."

"No problem.

"Are you going to tomorrow night's festival?"

Matthew nodded. "Patsy said it would be a good time."

"It is. I'll have a booth there."

"Will there be zombies and ghosts?"

She laughed. "You never know."

They stared at each other. The silence thickened, and for a moment, Matt envisioned a life with Natalie. It stretched out before him, a glittering promise of love and passion. He swallowed the sudden knot in his throat.

When the air conditioner kicked on, they both jolted, then grinned at each other sheepishly.

"I should go."

Matt didn't want her to leave. "I'll help you at the festival." The offer was casual and surprised him as much as it obviously surprised her. He cleared his throat.

"I'm going, anyway," Matt said. "And then I can fend off any ghost suitors who show up."

She laughed. "I feel bad about your pie and interrupting your meditation. I'm sorry about this," she paused, apparently trying find the right word, then said, "inconvenience."

"It's not inconvenient when a beautiful woman stumbles onto my porch. Only when she leaves too soon."

Natalie's brown eyes flared with desire.

His blood stirred. If the way she kissed was any indication of bedroom passion....*stop thinking that way, Dennison.*

"What time do you want me at your house tomorrow night?" he asked. "I insist."

"Okay." Natalie stood. "Festival starts at eight, and I need to be there at seven."

"I'll be early."

"Thank you. Good night, Matt." Her soft voice sent another hot-punch of lust into his gut. He blew out a breath.

"Would you like me to walk you home?"

"No. It's just a couple of blocks."

She went to the back door and opened it. As she slipped outside, he stood and watched through the window as Natalie picked up the abandoned cap and sauntered out of his backyard.

What was it about Natalie Haltom that drew him like a moth to a flame?

He shook his head. He should probably try meditating again, but what he really needed was a cold shower.

"TILDA REALLY BLEW it," said Kimmie. She ate some more popcorn, tossing a few kernels at Jenny who was busy painting her toenails purple.

"Hey, stop it. This stuff isn't dry yet."

"Where are the men?" she asked. "The dating throngs? The horny vampires!"

"Gross." Jenny looked up. "It's been a whole day, Kimmie. Maybe you should be glad nothing's happened."

Kimmie flipped restlessly through a tattoo magazine. Spending the night at Jenny's had been her idea. Mostly, it was self-preservation. She didn't actually want to be around when Tilda's spell started working.

Kimmie put aside the magazine. Doubt niggled at her. "I'm wondering...do you think I'm doing the right thing?"

"No," said Jenny. "Which I've told you about a

million times. Luckily, I'm just an unwitting accomplice." She capped the bottle and handed it to Kimmie. "It's too late now. The spell is cast. Your mother is going to kill you. But I'll sing *Amazing Grace* at your funeral."

"Don't you dare," huffed Kimmie. "It's *My Chemical Romance* or nothing at all." She considered it, and then added, "Or anything by *The Cure*."

"You'll be six feet under. What do you care?"

Panic fluttered in her gut, but Kimmie forced herself to relax. "Mom will be too in love to be mad at me. Besides, I'm her only child, and she wouldn't risk jail for the pleasure of murdering me. Jails are filthy, and Mom hates dirt."

"Whatever, dead girl."

CHAPTER FOUR

NATALIE ALMOST DROPPED the basket of cookies when the doorbell rang. She glanced at the clock. *Matt.* For some reason, he felt obligated to offer help, and she wasn't going to admit that the idea of spending the evening with him at the food festival thrilled her to no end.

As she went to answer the door, she swore she felt her heart pounded in an uneven rhythm. *Anxiety,* she thought. *You don't have a heartbeat.* The fact that she had seen Matthew Dennison gloriously naked set her non-existent pulse skittering.

"Get a grip," she muttered, smoothing the pink summer dress. She answered the door, pasting on a nervous smile.

"Hello, Natalie."

Matt's deep voice made her pulse leap. His green eyes reminded her of the weeping willow trees so prevalent in Broken Heart.

"It smells like cinnamon," he said.

Natalie's gaze swept over him. Dressed in a crisp short-sleeved green shirt and khaki walking shorts, Matt looked lean and healthy, giving "delicious" a whole new meaning.

"That was a hint," Matt said. "For breakfast."

She shook out of her weird revelry and realized she hadn't said a word since she'd opened the door. "I baked cinnamon rolls when I woke up."

"My favorite."

Leading the way to the kitchen, Natalie sucked in a breath and tried to center herself. She was obviously frazzled by the ghost proposal and zombie dance-off and Kimmie's potentially dating a pierced boy named Jackal. And, oh yeah, the stress of not picturing Matt naked.

Crap.

She was totally picturing Matt naked.

She used tongs to remove a thickly frosted roll, put it on a paper plate, and handed it to him.

He took a huge bite and chewed. After he swallowed, he looked at her. "That's the best cinnamon roll I've ever had."

She grinned. "I know."

Natalie faced the stove and finished putting cookies into the last basket. Naked Matt refused to leave her thoughts, and her body started to get the tingles. Matt probably knew sexual acts that were illegal in most countries.

The cookie in her hand snapped in two.

"Where should I start?" asked Matt.

Maybe the missionary position then you can work your way up to something more exotic, Natalie thought, but didn't dare say. Instead, she turned, holding the basket and giving him what she hoped was a cheerful expression. Pointing to the variety of prepared goods scattered on the counter, she said, "Start here. The minivan's unlocked. There's a special cart in the back to hold everything in place."

"Yes, ma'am." He winked at her and pleasure swirled through her.

Pretending nonchalance, she ignored the sudden pounding of her heart. His gaze would have melted frozen butter. He reached around her head and pulled out the ponytail holder. Her hair tumbled down. With gentle hands, he spread it out, touching her temples as his fingers combed through her hair. She shivered.

He stood back, looking at her as if he was an artist who'd just painted a canvas. "Beautiful." Whistling, he stacked three cake boxes in his arms and left.

THE FIRST COUPLE of hours passed in a flurry of Bloody Good Cupcakes (with O positive blood middles), Cat Cookies (with a sprinkle of catnip for the werecats), Chocolate Chewies (a favorite among the werewolves), and a bevy of cakes and cookies and pies for the humans and those among the parakind who liked less supernatural in their desserts.

All the residents of Broken Heart turned out for the festival. Games, rides, homemade treats, and the opportunity to dunk the werewolf king and his brothers in a hundred gallon tank of vanilla pudding were part of the fun. The evening would end with a huge fireworks display.

Matt had gone to the minivan to retrieve more baked goods. Ever so often, Kimmie and Jenny would appear and help out, but they would disappear again before she could have an actual conversation with them.

"Hello, babykins."

Natalie looked up from rearranging the cake selections and stifled a groan. "Don't call me babykins. What are you doing here, Jerry?"

He puffed up a bit, the awful blue jacket bunching around his waist. "Just wanted to see if the flesh-freak had broken your heart yet."

She sighed. "No," she said. "He hasn't."

His doughboy face fell, and he hung his head. The moonlight glinted off his bald spot. Poor guy. He was cute in a crestfallen sort of way.

"Here are your pies, darling," Matt said smoothly, putting the cherry cobblers on the table with a flourish. Startled, Natalie looked at Matt. *Darling?* Belatedly she remembered he'd engaged himself to her yesterday.

"Thank you, er, honey."

"No kiss?" Matt asked. He swept her into his arms and dipped her, brushing his warm lips over hers. Her body chilled, then heated. Delightful shivers scurried up her spine. He kissed her again, his mouth skimming over her jaw line and down her neck. Natalie clutched his shoulders. "Matt."

He looked at her, his gaze hungry. She forgot to breathe as she stared at him. He was pretending to want her for Jerry's sake—she knew that, but her knees didn't because they felt wobbly. Matt straightened, drawing her close to him. "Jerry. How's it going? Haunted anything recently?"

Jerry scowled at Matt, apparently intending to look ferocious, but to Natalie he looked more like a lost puppy who didn't know how to growl. Jerry faded away, but Matt didn't release her. He gathered her close, and she smelled his light cologne as she was pressed against his chest.

"He's gone," she said.

"I know." His smile was warm, but his gaze hadn't lost the fierce need she'd seen earlier. "You think that did the trick?"

It took a moment for her to find her voice. "Yes."

"Hey, Matt. Um, I hate to interrupt...whatever I'm interrupting, but do you mind filling in at the pudding tank for a little while?"

They turned and eyed one of the werewolf triplets. Natalie could never figure out which triplet was which, especially now with this one covered head to toe in creamy vanilla pudding.

"How did you get talked into that, man?" Matt laughed.

"Patsy can be very persuasive." He sent a pleading look to the psychic. "C'mon, please. Damian won't be here for another hour, and I literally have pudding coming out of my ears."

"All right, Darrius. But you owe me." Matt looked at Natalie. "You don't mind, do you?"

She laughed at the sudden picture in her mind of him covered in pudding. "Oh, no. I don't mind at all." She needed to text Jessica and Eva to go take him down, and then get photographic evidence. Jessica was a helluva shot, probably because she'd gotten so good at beating people up with her swords.

He squeezed her shoulder. "I'll be back later."

She watched as Matt and Darrius walked to the midway and admired the view from behind. The dunk tank was on the other side of the field, out of her sight unfortunately. Natalie rearranged all the items on the table, then dropped into a folding chair.

"Hey, Mom. How's it going?"

Kimmie's hair had lost the red food-coloring look. She'd chosen to wear a simple pair of stud earrings and no make-up. She wore a white T-shirt and jeans with a pair of high tops. Natalie felt her daughter's forehead. "What happened? Are you okay? Where's that purple thing with the silver spikes you were wearing?"

"Oh my God, Mom. I just felt like changing, okay?"

Natalie peered at her daughter's eyes. Solemn and sincere. And not to be trusted. Natalie looked at Jenny, whose expression was also too innocent. "What's going on?"

Kimmie and Jenny exchanged a look that made Natalie nervous. Then Kimmie shrugged. "Why go eat bad food or play a game? We'll watch the booth."

"You're volunteering to work?" She felt her daughter's forehead again. "You're definitely sick."

"I'm fine," she said with teenage exasperation. "Go have some fun already."

Like dunk a tall, handsome psychic in a tank full of pudding?

"All right."

"You should try the shaved ice, Mrs. Haltom," said Jenny. "There's a blood-coconut version that my mom really likes. Our friend Tilda is manning the booth. See? She's over there."

Natalie followed Jenny's pointing arm to a booth set up between two pecan trees and staffed by a young Goth girl making snow cones. Natalie felt peckish, especially since she'd had bagged blood today instead visiting her donor. "That sounds good."

She walked to the booth and stood in line.

"Hiya." Natalie turned and saw a man in a gray jumpsuit standing next to her.

He had the ghost glow.

Crap.

"You Natalie?"

She squinted at him. "Do you know Jerry?"

"Nope. I'm Tony Williams."

He reminded her a little too much of Norman Bates. His eyes were a dull brown, his teeth yellow, and his hair stringy. The jumpsuit he wore was stained and threadbare. She didn't like his vibe at all.

"Do you need help?" she asked. "Because I can send you to a good afterlife counselor."

"You wanted to date me," he said. "Here I am."

What the hell? Another ghost suitor? Ugh.

"You're dead," said Natalie.

"So are you, toots."

He did not just call me toots. "No, I'm undead. You're actually dead."

"Who cares? I don't see why you're complaining. You asked for dead guys."

"I did not."

"I'm doing you a favor," he said, flashing a yellowed smile. "Do you smoke?"

"No," she said. "Vampires don't have the lung capacity to inhale."

"Damn it. I'd kill for a *Marlboro*."

Natalie wondered if he really had killed someone for cigarettes. Tony's face narrowed to a point, and his eyes were small black beads. She had the feeling that being nice wasn't going to get rid of him.

"Go away," she said.

"I ain't leaving. This town is a dump, but it's better

than limbo." He leered at her. "You wanna do it?"

"Hey, shithead."

Natalie and the ghost turned. Queen Patsy stood there, hands on her jean-clad hips, her irritated gaze on Tony.

"Hey, toots," said Tony, turning his leer on Patsy. "You wanna do a threesome?"

"You are delusional." Patsy lifted her hand.

To Tony's surprise he was yanked upward.

"Back to where you belong, creep." She made a pushing gesture, and a small black hole appeared. Tony cried out as his ghostly form was sucked into it. Then the hole closed.

"Thanks," said Natalie. "I wish I could do that trick."

"You just have to marry a blood wolf and become queen of the vampires," said Patsy. "Easy peasy."

Natalie laughed.

"Mom!" came a chorus of children's voices. Patsy snapped her fingers. "I was so close to escape." She turned toward the four children and the man with moon-white hair coming toward her. As much as Patsy pretended to grouse about motherhood, Natalie knew how much she loved her family. Patsy waved good-bye and joined her brood.

Natalie was no longer in the mood for a shaved ice, so she returned to the booth.

The girls were staring at her open-mouthed and wide-eyed.

"What happened?" asked Kimmie. "You get in a fight with your invisible friend?"

"Ha, ha." Natalie waved off her daughter's concerns. "Don't worry about it. He was a confused ghost who Patsy sent back to the other side."

"What did he want?"

"To date me."

Jenny gasped, and then slapped a hand over her mouth. Kimmie had gone pale. Natalie eyed both of them. "Seriously, you two. What's going on?"

"Nothing," said Kimmie. "We promised Tilda we'd help her." She grabbed Jenny's arm and dragged her away.

Natalie stared after them.

Teenagers. Sheesh.

CHAPTER FIVE

MATT HAD GOTTEN dunked three times into the pudding tank thanks to Jessica Matthews. When his hour was finally over and Damian arrived, he struggled out of the vanilla goop. Jessica held up her iPhone and took a picture of him.

"Victory is mine," she yelled. Then she ran off before he could properly kill her.

Pudding coated every inch of his body.

Darrius took pity on him. The back seat of his car had been tarped up for this very reason, so Matt crawled in back and dripped like a slow-melting snowman on the way home.

By the time he showered, dressed and got into his car, another hour had passed. He was eager to get back to Natalie. Something inside him ached for her. His libido, probably.

Natalie was packing up when he arrived at the

booth.

"You're done?"

"The fireworks will start soon, and I'm nearly sold out of everything. But I did save you an apple pie." She picked it up and showed him, her smile wide and happy.

Then she was knocked sideways.

The pie flew out of her hands and splatted against a nearby tree.

Matt stared at the ghost cow. The damned thing had appeared out of nowhere and head-butted Natalie.

The cow mooed.

Natalie leapt behind Matt and clutched his shoulders. The cow snorted and pawed the ground.

"Nice cow," said Matt. "Good cow."

"Should we run?" asked Natalie

"Yes. We should definitely run."

"We can hide in the minivan."

Matt took off in a sprint, Natalie close on his heels. They jumped into the back of the minivan and slammed the doors shut.

"The universe doesn't want me to have pie," said Matt.

"Well, at least the universe isn't trying to kill you by cow."

They stared at each other, and Matt had an insane urge to kiss her. He'd tasted Natalie twice now, and wanted to do it again. And again. And again. Times infinity. He was attracted to her, damn it. He loved the cute little dip in her cheek and those nine freckles sprinkled across her nose. Oh, man. When had he counted her freckles?

"Should we check to see if it's gone?" asked

Natalie.

No, he wanted to say, *we should stay in here and make out.* He peered out the back door window. The cow had disappeared.

"It's safe," he said, and managed only mild disappointment.

Natalie popped open the door and looked around. "Let's hurry."

TILDA HAD CONVINCED her aunts to let Jenny and Kimmie spend the night. They were piled onto her bed looking at books Tilda had swiped from the witches' library.

"What is going on?" asked Kimmie as she leafed through *Spellcasting and The Urban Witch.* "Why are ghosts hitting on my mom?"

"Because," said Jenny, "you asked for dead guys. Ghosts are about as dead as you can get."

"I meant vampires," said Kimmie.

"Those are the undead," said Tilda. She was reading the contents page from *Witchcraft for Dummies.* "There's nothing in here about breaking love spells. You'd think that would be witchcraft one-oh-one."

"I thought love spells were among the no-nos," added Jenny. "Like raising the dead or rigging the lottery."

Tilda nibbled her bottom lip. "Well, not exactly. I mean, we were talking about dating, not falling in love."

Kimmie closed the book. "We have to fix this. Quick."

"Maybe we should just 'fess up," said Jenny.

"No!" Kimmie and Tilda yelled together.

Jenny rolled her eyes. "Fine. What's our plan of

YOU'LL UNDERSTAND WHEN YOU'RE DEAD

action?"

"We shouldn't have broken the circle," said Tilda. "That's probably how they got through in the first place." She sighed. "We need to find a binding spell, call them back, and stick them into the otherworld where they belong."

"All right. Bookmark anything that fits the bill," said Kimmie. "We have a lot of reading to do."

"Exactly how I like spending my Saturday nights," muttered Jenny.

Kimmie poked her best friend on the shoulder. "Shut up and read."

WHEN SHE PULLED into the driveway, Natalie felt exhaustion overwhelm her. Dawn was not that far away. She really wanted to take a hot bubble bath before she crawled into her coffin. Hah. Okay, it was a basement bedroom with no windows so the sunlight couldn't get to her.

Yawning, she exited the car and had barely shut the door when Matt pulled up in his black Jeep.

"Thanks for sticking around to help," she said as she opened the van's back doors.

"My pleasure."

Matt delivered the items from the minivan to the kitchen where Natalie put them away. Soon everything was done. Natalie offered Matt some iced tea, but he declined. They stood in the kitchen, listening to the clock tick, and Natalie wondered why Matt was still here. He could handle the sunlight, but she wouldn't be able to keep her eyes open. Vampires pretty much died during the day.

Natalie rubbed the back of her neck, refusing to look at him.

"How about a shoulder rub?"

Before she could say, no, Matt was behind her, his hands working magical circles. Kneading out the kinks, smoothing away tightness, helping her relax. She sighed deeply and leaned into the massage. Slowly, Natalie became aware of the change in Matt's touches, how his fingers stroked long lines down her back and up her arms. His warm breath stirred the hair at the nape of her neck.

His proximity did funny things to her stomach. She smelled his earthy, masculine scent, with a hint of vanilla left over from the pudding dunk. Her skin warmed where his hands touched her. Her body felt hot, tingly.

She stilled, afraid he wouldn't move—afraid he would. An aeon passed, and then Matt's hands trailed up her ribcage, stopping under her breasts. She felt the barest touch of his fingers. Her gasp was sharp.

"You're beautiful, Natalie," Matt whispered. His lips found the curve of her neck, and his tongue traced a path to her ear.

Natalie didn't want him to stop, even though it was foolhardy to even think of consummating their fake engagement. She turned in his arms and pressed against his chest. She heard his heart double its already frantic beat as he lowered his mouth.

His lips covered hers. His mouth was warm and tasted like coffee. When he teased her with his tongue, heat speared her. She felt drugged as her hands sought the firm muscles of his chest then crept higher to trace his collarbone. Her fingers slid into the soft thickness of his hair. Natalie deepened the kiss, pulling Matt closer, meeting his desire with her own. His groan sent sparks dancing down her spine.

She felt shattered and whole at the same time.

"Natalie." Matt pulled away, his heated gaze filled with a hunger that weakened her knees.

"We can't," she said.

"I know." Matt released her and retreated across the kitchen. She watched him run a hand through his hair. "I'm sorry."

"Me, too." Her chest constricted. Stupid vampire rules. She hadn't been touched or kissed or taken in far too long. Still, Natalie knew pleasure for the sake of pleasure would never be enough, so it wasn't like she would fall into bed with him even if she could. Probably. She knew her own heart too well. Even if she could have sex without mating to Matt, she wouldn't have a fling. Her emotions would get tangled into the sex. Where Matt was concerned, she knew hurt would be swift and deep when they couldn't make it work, whether he wanted it to or not.

"Good night, Natalie."

"Good night, Matt."

He nodded and left the kitchen. Moments passed before she heard the front door shut. The solid click echoed through the house.

Well, she thought. That was that.

CHAPTER SIX

THE DOORBELL RANG, and Natalie burrowed under the covers. She wasn't leaving bed today, she thought. She wasn't leaving bed ever again. The doorbell dinged two more times and Natalie groaned. She almost called out to have Kimmie answer it when she remembered her daughter had spent another night, well, day at Tilda's. If she didn't know better, she'd think Kimmie was avoiding her.

Bing Bong. Bing Bong. Bing Bong.

"All right!" Natalie huffed as she scrambled out of bed. She slipped into her pink house shoes, put on a robe, stomped up the basement stairs.

She shuffled to the door and flung it open. If it was Jerry, she was going to punch him in his doughy face. A short man with gray hair and a pencil thin moustache smiled at her. He held roses in one hand and box of candy in another.

And yeah, he was glowing.

"Natalie Haltom," he said in a timid voice. "I'm Kenny Rogers."

"You don't look anything like Kenny Rogers."

"Not the singer." He sighed. "It's unfortunate. I've spent my entire life and afterlife with that name. It's not easy living in that guy's shadow."

"Yeah. Sorry." She started to close the door, but Kenny shoved the roses into the gap.

"Mother so wants to meet you. She's waiting for us."

He brought his mother from the afterlife to go on a date? Was he crazy? Something inside Natalie broke. She stepped onto the porch, forcing the ghost the backwards, and shut the door behind her. *No ghosts allowed.* She didn't want Kenny or his mother showing up at her door again. So she latched on to the lie that worked so well before. "I'm engaged. My fiancé's name is Matt Dennison. And he's big. Huge. And jealous."

"Mother will be very disappointed." His gaze darted around as he scurried off the porch. "And really, you shouldn't be dating if you're engaged."

Duh.

Kenny disappeared, and Natalie slumped against the door.

"Hello, dearie!"

"Hi, Bettie."

The little old fae's eyes glinted gold. "Oh my dear. I couldn't help but hear you toss that ghostly gentlemen on his ear, poor soul." Bettie held up a spade and gardening gloves. "I was working on the rose bushes, and I just couldn't help ... Matt Dennison! You lucky thing! Now, have you talked to Lilly Halperger about your dress? She's the best seamstress in town, you know. And for the chapel, we'll have to do orchids. I love orchids. When did you say the date was?"

Natalie's thoughts whirled. "The date of what?"

Bettie beamed. "Why your wedding, of course!"

MATT HEARD THE phone ring as he exited the shower. The machine kicked on, then Natalie's voice filtered into the living room.

"I'm being kidnapped," she whispered. "By a crazed fairy in a wedding-planning frenzy. Please help me."

Her breathless, panicked voice clawed at him. He lunged for the phone. "Natalie? Are you all right?"

"I'll be downtown at Lilly's Dress Emporium. Get there and rescue me." The phone clicked, and Matt stared at the receiver for several seconds before hanging up.

He didn't know what had happened last night. He hadn't meant to let things get so heated, but Natalie was intoxicating. Her vulnerability had drawn him in. He'd wanted to soothe her, to show her ... well, that had been a mistake. He had no right to push the idea of a relationship on her. Especially when physical intimacy came at too high a price. Love with a vampire risked more than the heart, it risked the soul.

All the same, he needed to go rescue his damsel in distress.

WHEN MATT ARRIVEDhen Matt arrived at the Emporium, he entered the building and peered down the hall. People entered behind him, and Matt moved to the side to allow them to pass. He caught sight of Natalie rushing toward him.

She wore a short, white dress and sandals. Her toenails were painted pink. She'd worn her hair down, and it draped her shoulders. For a moment, he was utterly struck by her beauty, and it made him mute.

"Matt!"

His name was a rush of relief from her lips, but he wanted to hear her call his name in passion. Need tightened him. What was wrong with him? He wasn't going to seduce Natalie, despite the fact that he very much wanted her. Damn it. He'd already had this conversation with himself.

She took his arm and dragged him down the hall, through a dark, musty-smelling corridor and into a tiny room. "They're going to notice I'm missing soon," she said. "Something terrible happened this morning."

Matt covered her trembling hands. "What?"

"Another ghost wanting to date me. I, er, put him off by saying I had a fiancé." She nibbled her lower lip. "I didn't know that Bettie Smith was standing behind her rose bushes listening."

"Bettie?" Matt sucked in a breath. "The fae woman who headlines gossip faster than *TMZ*?"

Natalie nodded. "That's the one. She thinks we're getting married. I couldn't untangle myself long enough to explain it was a ruse, and the next thing I know, she's arranged a dress fitting and has ordered orchids for the church."

Natalie's cheeks flushed, and Matt tried not to think how lovely it made her look. She was still talking, and he realized he hadn't heard a word she'd said.

"Wait. What?" he asked. He swore she said something about a wedding.

"How would you feel about 'breaking up' before the wedding day?"

"We have a wedding day?"

"The twentieth. Of this month."

"That's next Saturday." He should be feeling a lot worse than he did just now. He should be annoyed that Natalie had carried the charade so far, but Matt couldn't work up sufficient anger. He frowned.

"Matt?"

"Okay, Natalie. We'll break up before the big day."

Her gaze softened. The gratitude in her dark eyes wrapped around him, and he wanted to kiss her stupid. He wanted her naked, writhing, and coming apart in his arms.

"We're going to have to sneak out," she said.

Matt guided Natalie out into the hallway, and they hurried toward the exit. Just as they reached the double doors, Matt heard, "There's the lovebirds now."

Natalie tensed then turned around, her troubled gaze colliding with his. He took her hand and held it tightly.

"Hello, darlings," Mrs. Smith trilled as she marched toward them. "Natalie, we must speak about the photographer. And I talked to Lenette at the Three Sisters Bed & Breakfast. She can host the reception. Isn't this wonderful?" She turned to Matt. "Our Natalie is quite a catch. Good thing you snatched her up when you did. I heard she's had men just knock, knock, knocking at her door!"

"Yes, well..." Matt noticed Bettie's smile had the force of a laser beam. It was bright and steady and aimed right at him. Natalie looked as stunned as he felt.

Bettie stood in front of them, her hands on her hips, looking at Natalie then Matt with narrowed eyes.

"We'll need pictures of the reception, too, I think. Matt, do you like purple? I'm terribly fond of purple ... do you like orchids?"

"What?" Matt asked, staring at the tiny, elderly woman. She looked remarkably like a Drill Sergeant—despite that peach hat covered with baby's breath that matched her peach dress.

"She's a black hole," Natalie warned in low voice. "She'll suck you in, and your will to live disappears."

"Of course, Kimmie will be the maid of honor," Bettie was saying. Her bird-like gaze landed on him. "Who will be the best man?"

Sweat broke out on his brow. He leaned down and said, "Let's run for it."

"It's not going to be that easy," Natalie whispered.

"The hell it's not."

A crowd of elderly women formed behind Bettie. Some held bridal magazines like shields. Where in blazes had they all come from? Matt eyed the old lady in front of them with a growing respect. The sergeant had called in the troops.

"I've gathered some of the girls to discuss the wedding arrangements. Natalie, do you have a few hours? We need to choose the music. How do you feel about the harpsichord?"

"What are you waiting for?" Natalie hissed in his ear. "Run!"

And Matt did, pulling his fake bride after him.

NATALIE AND MATT sat in the booth at the darkest corner of the café. The cracked vinyl seat wasn't comfortable, and it didn't help that Matt had squeezed beside her. He wore shorts, and the warmth from his flesh crept through her dress. She felt bathed in lava even though the air conditioner vent above their heads emitted an ice-cold breeze. And she didn't have blood circulation, so obviously her attraction to the psychic had reached nuclear proportions.

They each held a plastic menu to hide their faces.

"Did they see us?" asked Natalie.

"I think we're safe."

Natalie looked at Matt and shared a conspiratorial smile. His thick-lashed green eyes had flecks of gold around the pupils. Beautiful tiger-eyes. She finally managed to tear her gaze away from Matt's only to find it riveted to his sexy, full lips.

Matt leaned against the seat. His muscled, tan arm slid along the worn wood edge of the booth until she felt his fingers in her hair. His touch was light and disturbing. And wonderful.

"They'll find us in here," she said. "There are only two eating establishments in the entire town. We can't hide here forever."

"True. But we need nourishment if we're going to fend off Bettie and her battalion." He eased back, finally giving her some room. "Doesn't she remind you of rabid terrier?"

Natalie laughed. She shifted, grimacing when the vinyl stuck to her legs. Her short dress was useless protection against the seat.

"Hello, Natalie."

She looked up and sighed. "Jerry."

Without invitation, the ghost slid into the booth. His hound-dog features looked pastier in the bad light of the diner.

"Still getting married?"

"Yes," Matt said with a possessive edge.

Surprised, Natalie glanced at Matt. He put his arm

around her shoulders, fiddling with the spaghetti strap of her dress. The warm, lazy strokes tingled her skin.

Jerry's expression drooped.

"Well, here's the happy couple." Dottie the Ghost, a regular fixture in Broken Heart, pouted her bright pink lips in mocking accusation. She usually hung around Patsy, gave the vampire queen advice she didn't want, and caused trouble whenever she could. Dottie was determined to have a fun afterlife since her earthly life had been so crummy. After all, she'd been killed by her truck driver boyfriend.

"Please tell me Bettie isn't behind you," said Natalie.

"Don't worry, sweetie. They got distracted by the skeletons."

Natalie and Mattie stared at the ghost.

Dottie lit a phantom cigarette and blew out the smoke. It amazed Natalie how many habits spirits kept after they left their corporeal forms. "I'm guessing they came from the graveyard. There's not a lot meat left on 'em to be zombies." The voluptuous redhead slid into the booth next to Jerry. "What's shaking?" she asked the sullen suitor.

Jerry blushed.

Matt continued the soft touches, slipping a forefinger under her dress strap. Natalie felt a prickle zip down to her girly parts.

"So," said Dottie, her gaze taking in Matt's wandering fingers. "Are you waiting for the big day to do the nasty?"

Natalie nearly choked on her spit. "Dottie!"

"Well, you haven't bonded. I can always tell when vampires are mated." Dottie studied Jerry as the amorous ghost took in the redhead's beauty. She smiled winsomely.

"This is Jerry," said Natalie. "He's visiting."

"Well, that's just fine," purred Dottie. "You want me to show you the sights, honey?" She winked at him.

"Yes," said Jerry. "Definitely."

"Have fun, lovers," said Dottie. She put her hand on Jerry's rumpled jacket, and the two ghosts faded away.

"Poor Jerry doesn't stand a chance," Matt murmured.

The intent look in Matt's eyes belied the teasing tone of his voice. Natalie felt as if she'd been swimming in a strong current, and now the undertow was dragging her down.

Thankfully the food arrived, and Natalie concentrated on her chicken fried steak instead of Matt's disconcerting presence. Chicken fried steak, mashed potatoes dripping with homemade gravy, and thick, steamy biscuits were weaknesses of hers. Now that she was a vampire, there was no such thing as calories or bad-for-you food.

Without ceremony, Matt dug into his meatloaf.

They ate in silence, which held a thread of tension she didn't understand. Some time between hiding from Bettie and the conversation with Dottie, something between she and Matt had changed. She shoveled a particularly huge, dripping bite into her mouth.

"You look like a chipmunk," he said.

She chewed, barely able to swallow the meat. It finally went down, and she cut a smaller bite. "Shut up."

Matt laughed.

Natalie bit into a biscuit, sighing at its hot, fresh taste. "This is the best part of living in Broken Heart."

"Nat!"

Natalie looked up, her mouth full of biscuit and saw Jessica and Eva chugging toward them.

"You look like a chipmunk," said Jessica.

"Are you two getting married?" asked Eva. "Bettie Smith couldn't tell everyone fast enough."

"You'd think you'd tell us first," said Jess. "Have you had sex, yet?"

"Oh, dear lord." Natalie stared down at her plate.

"No," said Matt. "Look, it's a long story."

"Oh, you're telling us the story," said Jessica. "But you'll have to do it at the PPTA garage sale."

"PPTA?" asked Matt.

"Paranormal Parent-Teacher Association," explained Eva. "You're still going, right?"

Natalie had completely forgotten about the event, and that she was supposed to provide snacks and donate items. Shit.

"Yes," she said. "I'll be there."

Jessica stabbed a finger into the air. "You *both* will be there." She gave Matt a narrowed-eye look. "Don't you dare break her heart, or I will chop you into little pieces."

Matt swallowed the bite of food that had caught in his throat. Natalie took in his expression. He'd probably never noticed before how scary Jessica could be. He nodded.

"Good. Because no one would ever find your body."

"Noted," said Matt faintly.

CHAPTER SEVEN

"HOW DID MY own mother get engaged and not tell anyone?" Kimmie lamented as she, Jenny, and Tilda spread vinyl tablecloths over card tables. The annual PPTA garage sale was held at the Three Sisters Bed & Breakfast at sundown. Tilda's aunts had wasted no time putting the teens to work.

"Yeah. Makes the whole ghost dating thing really awkward," said Jenny.

"Look, your mom will be here soon," said Tilda. "We'll stick the juju bag on her person, and the ghosts will be repelled. Later on, we'll perform the binding ritual and get rid of the ghosts for good."

"I bet Patsy could get rid of them," said Jenny.

Tilda and Kimmie stared at her. "Are you *trying* to get us grounded?" asked Kimmie, horrified.

"We're going to be grounded anyway. Not one of us will walk away from this without parental fury being unleashed."

Tilda shook her head. "I got this. The ghosts disappear, your mom is safe, and hey, she has a man just liked you wanted for her."

Kimmie felt hot tears well up in her eyes. "I just wanted her to have someone good. She doesn't know that I know, but my dad is the one who got her killed. It's his fault she's a vampire. He fed her to his stupid boss!"

"Oh, Kimmie. I'm so sorry." Jenny hugged her.

Tilda patted her on the back.

She sniffled, feeling somewhat better...until she saw who was sauntering up the driveway, and had a moment of panic.

"Ohmigawd. It's him," said Kimmie.

"Mr. Dennison?" asked Jenny, turning around. "Oh, you mean loverboy."

"Shush."

"Whose loverboy?" Tilda craned to get a good look. "It's just Hayden Wickam. You like him? But he's such a nerd."

"Okay," said Jenny, pulling Tilda by the arm. "We're leaving." She dragged the girl all the way to the front porch and disappeared into the house.

Kimmie's heart pounded as the boy neared. He stopped, tucking his hands into his jean pockets. As he looked at her, a lock of brown hair fell across his forehead.

"Hello, Kim."

His use of her formal name sent a delightful shiver through her. Kimmie leaned against the table, crossed her arms, and pretended to be bored. "Hi, Hayden. What are you doing here?"

His mouth quirked. "Reporting for duty. Dad

insisted."

Kimmie flushed then ducked her head to hide her embarrassment. Hayden's dad was a local doctor for the human population in Broken Heart. "Oh, yeah. Help. Right." She felt stupid and disappointed. But why had she thought he would come just to see her?

"Yeah, help," he said. He stepped closer and brushed her hair away from her cheek. Kimmie looked into his brown eyes and felt like she was going to melt into a big, goopy puddle.

He leaned closer, and she could smell the peppermint on his breath. "Kim. I was wondering—"

"Yes?"

"The new theatre in town is playing *Shaun of the Dead.* And I know you're so cool and everything." His tone was teasing and nervous. "But I thought you might want—"

"Hayden." Dr. Elliot Wickham clasped his son's shoulder. "We're going to sticker the electrical items."

Hayden smiled at Kimmie and shrugged apologetically. As he turned to follow his dad, she snagged his T-shirt. "What were you going to ask me?"

"I'll ask you later."

Kimmie's heart skipped a beat as she watched Hayden walk up the driveway with his father. Her pulse continued to race. Hayden had been about to ask her to the show and had chickened out. Darn it. Why were boys such wimps?

MATT CARRIED ANOTHER box from Natalie's garage and shoved it into the back of the minivan. The night was typical of August in Oklahoma: hot and muggy. Even at night, it made no difference in temperature, but the heat enhanced the scent of fresh cut grass and honeysuckle that perfumed the air. He wiped the sweat from his forehead, and watched Natalie tirelessly lug an armful of clothing to the car. She flashed him a grin before returning to the garage.

He and Natalie seemed to be the only people outside. By the looks of it, everyone else had wisely decided to stay indoors. An odd quiet stole through the small neighborhood, making Matt feel as if he and Natalie were only human beings left on Earth.

Matt looked at Natalie, who flitted around the garage like a butterfly in a field. He watched her bend over a stack of magazines and saw the white dress rise... rise...he swallowed as the material dangled over her derriere, swinging provocatively as she dug around in the pile of stuff. She turned, holding a gold candlestick holder as triumphantly as an Olympic athlete holding the Torch.

He had an insane urge to flip up that damn dress and— "Do you want to take a break?" he called out.

Natalie put the candlestick in a carton and walked toward him. "There's still stuff to do," she said, handing him the box.

He put it in the van for her, but before she could get away, he grasped her by the elbows and drew her close. "C'mon. Even vampires should take a break from hard labor."

"I'm a vampire *and* a mom, which means I really don't get any breaks." All the same, she leaned into his embrace, apparently content to be in his arms.

Just one taste. He'd take just one tiny taste of Natalie Haltom. Before he could stop himself—as if he wanted to—he pressed his mouth at the hollow of her throat, and kissed the pale, cool flesh. She inhaled sharply and grasped his shoulders. Matt nipped kisses up her neck to her jaw, flicking his tongue on her skin.

"Matt, please."

"Please what?" he whispered. He pulled her closer, looking at her wide amber eyes. He lowered his head and traced her trembling lips. When his tongue demanded entrance, she yielded, and met him with her own tentative touches. Desire twisted inside him, a spiraling need that claimed him until all he could feel, all he could *breathe*, was Natalie.

She broke the kiss and sagged against the back of the minivan. He put his arms on either side of her head and leaned down, feathering kisses along her cheek to the corner of her mouth.

"I want you, Natalie," he said in a jagged voice. He took her lips in a fierce possession, showing her with his mouth what he wanted to do with her body.

Her hungry little moan destroyed his already flagging willpower. Somehow his shirt had become unbuttoned and Natalie's cool, eager hands stroked his chest. The sensible voice in his head cited all the reasons he couldn't make love with Natalie Haltom, but she chose that moment to explore the waistband of his shorts, and he forgot everything but the woman in his arms.

"Hey, folks," a man's jolly voice chortled.

Matt and Natalie jumped apart as if electrocuted. Matt started to turn, to protect Natalie's disheveled appearance from the rude bastard who'd spoken but realized his own hard evidence would be more difficult to hide.

Natalie peeped over his shoulder. "Oh dear."

Matt turned, strategically placing Natalie in front

of him and looked at the balding, overweight man grinning at them.

"Y'all aren't even newlyweds yet," he said with a gleam in his eyes. "Better keep to hand holding in public, if you know what I mean." He winked.

"Who the hell are you?" asked Matt, irritated by the man's jovial interruption.

Natalie whispered, "He's the mayor."

"I didn't know Broken Heart had a mayor," said Matt.

"Oh, not of Broken Heart, son. I'm the mayor of the Little People. We have a village out past the barn on Simone and Brady's property. "Have you met Flet? He's the pixie. Set us up right fine."

"You're not little," said Matt.

"Oh, no. I'm not. I wouldn't be, now would I?"

"Um … no?"

"Mayor Hewitt Twinkletoes," the man said, presenting a chubby hand. Matt maneuvered around Natalie and accepted the Mayor's handshake. "Most folks call me Hewie."

Twinkletoes? "What can we do for you?" asked Matt.

"Glad you asked, Mr. Dennison, glad you asked. We little people have heard of your impending nuptials. I have to say, well-timed. Well-timed, indeed, sir. Perfect as a matter of fact." The mayor's smile was wide and toothsome.

Uneasiness swept over Matt in a cold wave.

"Your wedding falls on one of our most cherished holidays, and there's nothing the Little People like better than celebrating fertility."

"Fertility," said Matt flatly.

"And marriage," Hewie hurriedly added. "Of

course, marriage. That's the most important part for you humans, and uh, vampires. Our community would like the opportunity to help you celebrate your hundred years of marital bliss." The Mayor paused and flashed another terrifying smile. "We'd consider it a great honor if you and Natalie would marry in our sacred space—and that you might take on the spirits, as it were, of our god, the Great Glimmerrod and our goddess, Her Supreme Sparklenose."

Matt opened his mouth, but no words came out. He looked down at Natalie, and her expression could only be called "flabbergasted."

"It's so kind of you to think of us," said Natalie. She cleared her throat.

The mayor held up his hands. "Now, don't say no until you've had some time to consider it. We do have incentives. One wish each and a sack of gold. Long as we can pry it from the leprechauns. They like to hoard, you know."

"Why us?" asked Matt. "Wouldn't you prefer your own little people for such a ceremony?"

Hewie had the grace to look uncomfortable. "We would, we would. But we've had some dissension among our folks about who gets to play the parts of Glimmerrod and Sparklenose. It was finally decided that the only way to make it fair—was to not pick anyone from our community."

"Mr. Twinkletoes," said Matt. He paused, but he was uncertain what to say next.

The mayor offered another wide grin. "You two think about it now. I'll see you at the picnic later on tonight, and you can give me your answer then."

He turned around and trundled off before Natalie or Matt could gather their composure.

NATALIE PACED BACK and forth in her living room. She flashed a look at Matt, who reclined on the couch rubbing his temples. God, how had they gotten into this mess? *I will never lie again,* she swore.

She stopped wearing tread in the carpet and closed her eyes. She'd compounded Matt's lie when she tried to use it to ward off Kenny Rogers. She would just have to take her lumps like a woman. She'd survive. "I'm so sorry, Matt. I'll just admit that it's all a big sham. I'll call Bettie right now and confess."

"It's not your fault this whole town is crazy, Natalie." He stood up and gathered her into his arms. "But there's still time to break up publically, and until then..."

Natalie didn't pull away, even though she knew she shouldn't enjoy the way he held her. She felt safe, protected. She swallowed the knot in her throat. Matt had never really been hers, so why was she so stricken with the thought of ending a nonexistent relationship?

"At the PPTA garage sale tonight?" she suggested.

Matt's arms tightened around her. "The mayor mentioned something about a picnic."

"The witches host a barbecue after the garage sale. Should we do it then?"

"Yes," Matt answered. He kissed the top of her head, and then let her go. He turned around quickly, too quickly, and left the house. She heard him putting the last of the boxes into the minivan.

His kisses, his touches had told her such wonderful things—that she was beautiful and sexy. She steeled herself against the hurt gathering in her chest. *It is for the best,* she told herself. *So buck up, woman. Matt isn't yours.*

And he never will be.

CHAPTER EIGHT

NATALIE LOOKED AT the flat tire and kicked it. She and Matt had been headed to the bed and breakfast, about ten miles outside of town, for the garage sale when the tire blew. Though the road was paved, potholes existed every five or so feet—a typical condition of Oklahoma streets. However, the jumbo hole that had caused the flat happened to be on the stretch of land lacking any civilization. Thick, dense woods shadowed both sides of the road. At this rate, she'd never get to the garage sale. On the up side, she wouldn't have to deal with Bettie, who'd probably picked out the music, the bridesmaid dresses, and the flowers already.

Neither one of their cell phones worked, either. They were in some kind of dead zone that had nothing to do with zombies, vampires, or ghosts. She scanned the forest, hoping to catch a glimpse of Matt. He'd excused himself and gone off into the woods because men had the ability to pee standing up. In other words, wherever they wanted. Unfortunately, the spare was flat too.

Slumping against the van, she tucked a few loose wisps of hair behind her ear. Maybe Matt would have an itch to loosen it again. *Gawd*. She had to stop thinking about him—and wanting the man to touch her. He was handsome, nice, and he put a spring in her step. She and relationships didn't mix. And the last one, ended with her becoming undead. Which was every reason for her to run for the hills. *Kill me once, shame on you. Kill me twice, shame on me.* And she was doing exactly that, running, well, not for the hills, but to the local PPTA Garage Sale so she could dump Matt and.... Her heart ached with a sense of loss. Impossible, of course. She was just being silly. After all, what had there been to lose?

Sighing, she walked to the driver's side, climbed in and pretended not to wait for Matt. She checked the hazard lights, wiped the dust from the dashboard, and drummed fingertips on the steering wheel. After what felt like hours, which in fact had only been about five minutes in Natalie's estimation, Matt emerged from the woods.

Natalie watched his lean-hipped walk as he casually approached the minivan. His hands were tucked into the pockets of his shorts and his caramel brown shirt clung to his broad shoulders. He halted in front of the van, and removed his shirt, using it to wipe the sweat from his body.

Zowie. She wondered if he'd done it on purpose to get her attention. Probably, but did she really care?

Nope. His broad chest and flat stomach testified to Matt's use of weights. Brown curls sprinkled his chest, narrowing into a line that disappeared into his shorts. *You've already seen him naked.* Okay. Okay. Be calm. A hot, intense thread of desire weaved through her—silky strands of want and need arrowed down to her core. Her nipples tightened and beaded against the soft cloth of her dress.

The feeling burgeoned, making her throat dry and her hands shake. Lust. This was pure lust. She wet her lips, watching as he ran his long fingers through his hair. Then he stopped suddenly and raised his head to look at her. His predatory stare reminded her of a lion who carefully watches his prey before pouncing on the hapless creature.

Slowly, he walked to her opened window and leaned inside, his green eyes dark, hungry.

"What are we going to do since the spare's flat," Natalie said, unable to look away from his gaze.

"I'm sure we can think of something." He leaned into the open window.

Natalie's lower bits clenched with sudden need, but she tried to stay strong. "I thought we could, um, walk or try to flag someone down."

He reached in and caressed her cheek, stroking a thumb sexily across her lower lip. "Good idea."

She swallowed hard, her voice squeaky when she spoke. "Matt, it doesn't sound like you care too much about our predicament."

A corner of his mouth lifted. "I'm in a predicament myself."

She blinked. "What predicament is that?"

"I don't know what this is between us. It's the damnedest thing I've ever experienced." She saw him look at her stiff nipples straining against the white material. His jaw clenched. "I get all flustered and warm and..." He cast a downward glance at his groin. "...hard just thinking about you, sweetheart. You turn me on in so many ways, I've lost count."

His words undid her knots of doubt and turned her insides to warm mush. Matt wanted her. As a woman. With no expectations or demands.

"It's lust," she blurted.

"Yes, it's certainly that." His gaze returned to her breasts. He poked his head through the window and kissed her. Natalie tingled all the way to her toes. She wanted his mouth on her breasts. On her stomach and thighs and ... everywhere. She clutched the steering wheel harder.

Matt backed out of the window and opened the driver side door. "I want you," he said in a hoarse voice.

Natalie turned in the seat toward him, and yelped when he pulled her out of the van. Before she could analyze her actions, she'd wrapped her legs around his thighs. He lifted her up and pressed her back against the side of the van. On impulse, she lowered the strap of her dress with only the barest of hesitation when she exposed the top of her breast, her nipple still hidden.

With a low growl, Matt leaned forward and nipped her flesh, trailing a wet line. Gently he lowered the material just enough to tease the taut peak with his tongue. Then he suckled. Natalie arched against the side door, moaning at the pleasure Matt created. His hand found her other breast, his fingers cupping, kneading, and pinching. Liquid heat scorched her, pooling in the center of her thighs.

She cried out when he stopped. She looked at him and noticed his unsteady breathing. He wrenched the side door open. "Inside," he demanded, his tone hot with need.

"Yes," Natalie agreed. "God, yes."

The boxes were in the way, but before she could protest, Matt was yanking them out with one hand and shoving her into the van with his hips.

Natalie didn't think, didn't analyze, didn't care. Her body buzzed with an intensity she didn't recognize. She scrambled into the back, pushing anything left out of the way, and found an open spot between two boxes. She'd barely lie down on her back when Matt slid on top of her, his arousal hard against her belly.

"What are we doing?" she whispered.

"No mating," he promised. "I just want to give you pleasure. I need to give you pleasure, Natalie. I want to touch you and taste you. I won't take more than you can offer, but let me do this for you. For us."

Without waiting for her answer, his kisses claimed her. His mouth courted her with fierce need and raw desire. He wrenched himself away, his breath heavy as he stared at her. Then he slid lower and pushed up her dress, exposing her pale thighs and wet panties. Natalie squirmed. He promised no mating, but it left all kinds of other possibilities. His kisses on her hips made her frantic.

"A white thong? Woman, you're going to give me heart failure." He eased them off, and then parted her with gentle fingers. When she felt his warm mouth against her, she bucked and pushed at his head. Matt took her hands and placed them on the inside of her thighs. "Open for me," he whispered.

Natalie did, her body tight and needy as she lifted her knees and parted her legs for him. He kissed her very core, and then suckled the tiny nub. Raw pleasure jolted through her. Matt's hands grasped her hips and drew her close as he sucked, licked, kissed her sensitive bundle. Whatever he was doing with his mouth created a maelstrom of wicked, intense feelings, and Natalie's body begged for more.

Her hands dove into his hair, pulling him still closer.

"Let go, Natalie," Matt said against her sensitive flesh. She shivered. "I want to taste all of you, sweetheart."

Natalie felt his mouth fully on her, his tongue doing wondrous, unimaginable things. She matched Matt's flicking tongue with tiny movements of her own. The feeling built, rising, until she was straining, reaching...she arched against Matt, who continued to nip and lick and suck.

Natalie burst into a thousand stars.

MATT GROANED AS Natalie throbbed against him, her thrust his tongue inside her, tasting her orgasm as her scream of pleasure echoing through the tight confines of the minivan. He was relentless in bringing her to climax, not just once, but multiple times, wanting her to come so hard and so fast, she wouldn't ever forget his loving.

When she couldn't take any more pleasure, when it edged this side of painful, he savored one last taste, and then raised himself above her, his arousal still imprisoned in his shorts.

He gave her a moment, and when she recovered

her wits, she looked at him, eyes wide, and said, "That was amazing."

"You are a passionate woman, Natalie." He kissed her then whispered against her mouth, "Unzip my shorts, sweetheart."

Her eager hands obeyed him, and Matt groaned when he felt her fingertips lightly brush him through the briefs. He quickly shed them and gathered her close, kissing her, touching her, stroking her. He folded the top of the dress down and looked at her breasts. Firm and beautiful, the coral tips puckered in invitation. So he bent and took a nipple in his mouth, teasing it, pulling and sucking as she began to stroke his length.

Natalie quickened her pace on his shaft, and her moan when he sucked her nipple hard nearly broke him. He wanted to plunge into her moist heat, but kept his movements slow and deliberate. *No mating,* he reminded himself. It would tie her to him in a way that wouldn't be fair to Natalie. No matter what he wanted.

Her hands were everywhere, his chest, in his hair, his arms and shoulders ... his painful arousal. She drove him wild, distracted him from the gentle seduction he wanted to give her. When her hand slipped off his erection and curled around his buttocks, urging him toward her, he slid along and between the wet folds of her womanhood, groaning at the slick, wonderful feel of her.

It felt so good.

Too good. He stopped and cursed. He was rock-hard with want and need. He looked down at Natalie and saw his own passion reflected in her eyes. Oh God. What they were doing. He wanted to thrust inside her, to take her hard, and make her his own. But he'd made a promise. All those self-lectures about why he couldn't make love with Natalie incinerated under the heat of their joining, but he resisted completing the mating. Instead, he moved slowly, his cock rubbing against her clit. It had been awhile since he'd been intimate with a woman and he relished the sweet feel of Natalie's flesh.

He felt her thighs tremble and knew she was close to another orgasm. Both pain and pleasure swirled through him. She moaned and arched against him, offering her breasts to his eager mouth. As he teased her sensitive flesh, he felt the throbbing begin and her fingernails dug into his shoulders.

"That's it, sweetheart," he said softly, coaxing her higher. She shattered against him, and he pushed hard against her vibrating heat, panting, as his release shattered him, too.

AFTER THEY'D CLEANED up, they got into the front seats. Natalie turned on the van so they could enjoy some air conditioning.

Matt watched her tap buttons on her phone, carefully and obviously avoiding eye contact with him, but it was useless. No cell signal in this patch of Oklahoma woods, and every time she glanced his way he was staring at her. He couldn't help it. She was beautiful, and in the afterglow of their love making, her pale skin was almost flushed.

A honking horn's rendition of "Love Me Tender" startled Matt out of his thoughts. A pink Cadillac the size of a yacht pulled in front of the minivan.

Natalie stared at the car, and then turned to Matt. "You see that, right? I'm not delusional from the heat?"

"Nope. It's there."

"Hey there, folks," yelled a cheerful male voice. "Y'all need some help? I saw the flat tire."

Matt turned and looked at the hefty gentleman dressed in a white jewel-studded cowboy suit. Even though it was nighttime, the man wore diamond-shaped purple sunglasses. His ten-gallon hat had "The King" emblazoned on it in big gold letters. Lowering the window, Matt said, "Can you give us a ride? Our destination isn't too far."

"Sure, sure," the man said. "My Caddy has room for a whole orchestra."

They quickly loaded the Cadillac's cavernous trunk with the garage sale items. Natalie slid into the front seat, and Matt got into the back. Everyone clicked on their seatbelts. Then Frank "Elvis" Schmidt turned on "Jailhouse Rock" and spun gravel as he maneuvered onto the road. Natalie gave him directions, and he flashed them a huge grin. "I'm new in town," he said. "Not much call for vampire Elvis impersonators. So here I am, in Broken Heart. And I'm all shook up." He grinned. "In a good way."

Matt exchanged an amused glance with Natalie.

"So y'all married?"

"Er, no," Matt said. "My name's Matt Dennison and this is Natalie Haltom."

"Hey now, darlin', I'm just so lonesome I could cry! I ain't nothing but a hound dog, a good old boy looking for love—"

"In all the wrong places?" Matt supplied, unable to resist.

"Wrong song, son," Frank said heartily.

Soon they turned onto the road that led to the bed

and breakfast. As they pulled into the huge yard already filled with cars, Matt spotted Kimmie talking to Hayden. They exited the car, and Matt took Natalie by the elbow. She turned to Frank. "Thank you so much for the ride."

"You're welcome, little mama." He helped them unload the car, and then he wandered away.

"Mom!"

Matt and Natalie turned. An excited Kimmie and Jenny rushed to them. "I can't believe this! It's so great." She danced a jig around Natalie and hugged her mother.

Then Matt found Kimmie's arms wrapped around him. "Mr. Dennison is gonna be my stepdad!"

CHAPTER NINE

NATALIE FELT AN icy wave of dread wash over her. They'd taken this fake engagement way too far. Why hadn't it occurred to her that Kimmie would know about the engagement? She glanced at Matt and saw his shock. Their little white lie had coalesced into a huge catastrophe. The excitement dancing in Kimmie's eyes inflated Natalie's guilt.

"Lovebirds!" trilled Bettie. "We have so much to discuss." The tiny old woman was attached to Frank's chubby arm. "This man is not only a devoted fan of the King, he's got a night club act...and he's a preacher. Isn't this fabulous? Why, Matt and Natalie, you're going to be married by Elvis at the Little People fertility festival! It's all so perfect!"

Frank struck a pose. "Uh thank ya, thank ya very much."

Natalie gaped with shock then started to laugh. She couldn't stop, and she knew she sounded like an out-of-control clown, but the ridiculous situation overwhelmed her. *This is hysteria*, she told herself, but aloud she said, "It gets worse and worse, doesn't it?" And she laughed some more. So hard, in fact, she snorted and gasped and coughed.

"Mom? Are you okay?"

"Kimmie, go get your mother some water," Matt said. He lifted her onto the Caddy's trunk. "Are you all right, Natalie?" he murmured, pushing her hair behind her ear.

"Nope."

Bettie, Frank, and Jenny crowded around Matt. Natalie closed her eyes against their concerned expressions. She'd been such an idiot. Why had she let it get this far? She opened her eyes just as Kimmie appeared with a paper cup of water. She gratefully drank the water and handed the cup back to her daughter.

She didn't know what to say, what to do. She looked at Matt.

He turned around. "Everything's fine," he said. "Please don't be concerned. Its just pre-wedding jitters."

Everyone nodded and dispersed except for Kimmie. Natalie squeezed her daughter's shoulder. "It's okay, "she told Kimmie, "Go on. I'll talk to you later."

Kimmie kissed Natalie on the cheek. "I love you, Mom. I just want you to be happy."

Natalie looked at her only child's sweet face and felt her heart turn over in her chest.

"I'll take care of her," Matt said softly. His words

gutted Natalie. They were breaking up tonight, and here he was telling her daughter he'd take care of her. It was impossible. The whole situation.

Kimmie nodded and walked toward the garage sale, looking back at Natalie every few steps. Her daughter's obvious concern tore at her.

Matt put his arms around Natalie. She snuggled into his warm embrace, feeling like a leech sucking out all his comfort, but she couldn't pull away. Matt didn't seem in any hurry to end the hug either, so she stayed against his chest remembering how good his body had felt against hers and listening to the sound of his thudding heart.

Natalie thought about the days after her ex-husband had left. After she'd gotten over the shock of his abandonment so he could join Children of the Night, AKA a vampire cult, she'd felt a vast relief. She'd savored having a Ronald-free life. Her and Kimmie started building new memories, better experiences. Then Ronald went and ruined it by kidnapping Natalie and handing her over to Phil the vampire as a sacrifice.

Dark One, my ass. Phil had been a ridiculous man, all self-important and pompous because he'd found a bunch of jerk humans who would worship his undead ass. She didn't feel one bit bad that Ash, the detective who freed her, killed the bastard, for the second and last time, good and dead.

She looked at Matt and placed a gentle kiss on his cheek. "Thank you." He looked startled, but then kissed her lightly on the lips.

"I know it's important that we end this marriage facade, but I don't want to fight. Not tonight."

Natalie didn't want to stage a fight, either. Not

ever. She wanted to live in this new place she'd found with the psychic, but she couldn't expect him to give up his life to be with her. He was alive, and she was undead. Even if he wanted to date her, how could she expect him choose between becoming a vampire or growing old when she could not?

THE GARAGE SALE closed. Natalie and Matt had separated, though it seemed every time she sought him in the crowds, she found his gaze directed at her. He'd smile and she'd smile, too, feeling like a giddy teenager.

Speaking of giddy teenagers, Natalie realized Hayden—son of Dr. Wickham—was the object of her daughter's affections if the way they flirted was any indication. And that meant *Jack-hole* was not her daughter's crush. *Yay.*

The barbecue geared up, and Natalie, for the first time this night, was told to go away and stop helping. Her fake, impending marriage had sent the town into a weird frenzy. She'd received congratulations and advice all evening, and she was sure Matt had received the same. It worried her. She squared her shoulders. She'd made her bed—she'd damn well lie in it. Especially if Matt was in it with her.

Matt. He had her twisted inside and out. She knew he cared for her, and she knew he wanted her. She couldn't help but think about what life, or unlife, would be like with Matt. She envisioned laughter. Hot sex. Cozy nights. Affection. Support.

Love.

To her ex-husband, she'd always been a wife, a homemaker. He'd never seen her as a true partner, he'd never given her credit for her intellect or asked about her dreams or tried to understand what was in her heart.

But Matt did all those things without even trying.

MATT WATCHED NATALIE bend over the table, tugging at the edge of the vinyl cover. Once again, the dress fluttered provocatively, and now that he knew just what pleasures awaited him under that dress, his response was sudden and embarrassing.

He wanted her. In so many ways. When she wiggled, he couldn't stand not being next to her, not touching her, anymore. Looking around, he noticed almost everyone except Kimmie and Jenny had convened to the backyard for the barbecue. Then that kid Hayden appeared and escorted the girls around the house.

Natalie was alone. Finally.

He walked next to her and put his arms around her. He trailed soft kisses on her neck.

Her head lolled back, giving him better access. "You taste good," he murmured. He pushed his arousal into her stomach and cupped her buttocks, pulling her to him even closer.

She pressed tiny kisses on his jaw and neck. Each touch from Natalie was torture. And he loved it.

Matt pressed his lips against hers, and she opened her mouth to him, her hands creeping up into his hair. After a long moment of drinking from her, of tasting her, Matt dragged himself away.

Natalie's dazed smile ripped at his flagging control.

Matt grabbed her hand. "Let's go eat before I do something stupid."

"Yes," she agreed, but he could see the reluctance in her eyes.

"Maybe we could..."

Unfortunately, before he could say more, well-meaning folks separated Matt and Natalie and dragged them toward the picnic. Natalie managed to escape first, and she gestured to a secluded area. He nodded and tried, in vain, to push through the group of well-wishers.

"Thanks, everyone, really," Matt said. "But I need to get some food."

He turned, not liking the knowing grins he received. How would these people react when he and Natalie ended their engagement? An unsettling emotion niggled at him. The townspeople would eventually accept that he and Natalie were not getting married. He headed toward the buffet table, his stomach growling. The smells of roasted chicken, baked beans, and mustard potato salad made him salivate. He saw Natalie on the other side of the table with two plates. She indicated one plate was his. Then she smiled that same smile he'd seen all day. She had secrets in her eyes—secrets only he knew. It pleased him—far too much.

Kimmie stepped into his path. "Mr. Dennison?"

He gestured toward the wooded area close by. "We can talk over there."

They walked to the edge of the forest. At least hundred people milled about, eating, drinking, talking, and laughing. Men and women engaged in a horseshoe contest. Children played tag. Babies cried. Strung-up paper lamps lighted the yard. Matt enjoyed watching the activities for a moment, and inhaled the scents of the night. Any outsider who might happen upon this gathering wouldn't suspect that these townsfolk were vampires, werewolves, fairies, and witches.

"What's up, Kimmie?"

She withdrew a small bag from her pocket and handed it to him. "I made this for Mom. I was hoping you would give it to her." She glanced behind her, and said, "Do you think she's okay?"

"Yes," Matt replied. "What is this?" He glanced at the tiny silk bag sitting in his palm.

"My friend Tilda says it brings luck." Kimmie shrugged. "I thought maybe Mom would like it."

"So why don't you give it to her?"

Kimmie's gaze skittered away. "It's better if you do. Mr. Dennison, I just wanted her to be happy. I didn't know you two were dating already. Mom never said anything."

Matt felt his gut clenched. No wonder Natalie had second thoughts about the fake fight. What would Kimmie do when she realized Natalie and Matt weren't bonding at all? He looked down at the bag. What would it hurt to bring Kimmie's gift to her mother?

"I'll take it to her," said Matt.

"Thanks." Kimmie smiled shyly at him. "I don't know how you guys got together—but I'm glad. Mom's had a rough go. My dad..." Her words trailed off, but he could see shame and guilt in Kimmie's expression. Shame and guilt she hadn't earned, but still felt. Sometimes that happened when the people we loved or were supposed to love us turned out to be terrible and awful. With his ex-fiancé, he'd felt some of that responsibility as well.

Matt felt shamed now. Damn. Natalie had been right—the situation kept worsening. What had started out as a little lie to deflect an amorous ghost had turned into a complete catastrophe. He didn't want to hurt any one with their deception. Not the excited townsfolk, not Kimmie, and most of all, not Natalie.

Kimmie gave his arm a quick squeeze, and with a little wave, she took off. He watched her join Jenny and Tilda. All three girls looked at him expectantly. Then they turned away and bent their heads together, having some kind of whispered conference.

Matt pocketed the luck bag.

Teenagers were weird.

"HI, NATALIE,"

Natalie looked up, a chicken leg poised before her lips. Jerry floated above her, smiling shyly. He looked different—less sad, she supposed. She put the leg down and gestured for him to sit on the blanket she'd arranged for her and Matt—far away from everyone else.

"I figured you'd be here," he said as he sat beside her. He floated a few inches above the ground. He avoided looking at her, instead directing his gaze at the people milling around the yard. "I wanted to tell you that I think you and the flesh-freak make a good couple." He glanced at her. "Dottie set me straight, you know." He blushed. "She's quite wonderful."

"So you and Dottie…"

His doughy face reddened as he blushed harder.

Natalie pressed her lips together to keep from laughing. Poor Jerry was adorable in his own pathetic way. She patted his shoulder. "I'm happy for you. Does that mean you're staying?"

"Dottie's working it out with the queen. She says Patsy will probably agree to me hanging around since it'll mean Dottie won't bug her as much."

This time, Natalie laughed.

Jerry snickered, too. He shook his head. Then his expression turned somber. "I really don't know how many of us escape through the portal," he said. "But I do know that something else came with us. Ghosts aren't all harmless, you know."

Natalie thought of the disgusting Tony. "We've dealt with one of those already."

Jerry nodded. "The portal's closed. I mean, Patsy has the ability to send us back to limbo, but who knows how many ghosts even stayed around here."

"You mean some of them left Broken Heart?"

Jerry shrugged. "You asked for a love life and said you wanted dead guys. That was enough to have several of us lining up."

"But I didn't ask for any of those things. I didn't open a portal. And I didn't want a love life."

"Looks like you found one anyway." Jerry offered her another shy smile as he cast a furtive glance in Matt's direction. "Just be careful, Natalie."

"I will." She squeezed Jerry's hand. "I'm happy for you and Dottie."

"Thanks." He floated into a standing position. "Good-bye, Natalie. See you around."

She nodded her good-bye then picked up the chicken leg. After taking a bite, she put it on the plate, kicked off her shoes, and stretched out. She wasn't hungry anymore. The idea of her and Matt's charade ending now left her empty ... like a hole that could never be filled. Where was Matt? She'd been sitting there for half an hour, anticipating his arrival.

She set aside her plate of food and tried not think about ghosts, dating, or portals. The area she'd picked was isolated enough to hear nature over the dull conversations coming from the other picnickers. She stretched out on the blanket, closed her eyes, and listened to the chirping of crickets and the wind rustling through the trees.

And tried to shake off the foreboding that squeezed her stomach.

KIMMIE SETTLED AGAIN the tree, morosely watching everyone enjoy themselves. Man, she'd screwed things up. She wiped the tears from her eyes. Mom would probably kill her for trying to use magic to create a love life for her. The idea seemed dumb now.

"What's wrong, Kim?"

Hayden sank down beside her, his concern evident in his brown eyes.

"Nothing," she said, turning away. *Figures he shows up when I'm bawling like a big baby.* "Just go away."

He touched her cheek. "You're crying."

"Duh," Kimmie said. "You've discovered the secret of the century."

Hayden chuckled. "I love it when you do that."

Kimmie swiped at her face. "Do what?"

"Use sarcasm. It means something's got your goat."

His grin flashed in the darkness. Kimmie felt the bottom drop out of her stomach. He was so cute. Darn him, anyway. Why couldn't he go away and let her be miserable? "You've got me all figured out, Hayden."

"No, not really." He leaned forward, brushing the hair from her eyes. "I don't have you figured out at all. But I'd like to." He caressed her cheek, closing in until his lips were a mere inch from hers. "I've been meaning to ask you—"

"Yes," Kim breathed.

Hayden looked surprised, then pleased. His grin returned. "Do you even know what you said yes to?"

Kimmie's heart pounded. Boys! Didn't he know how close he was? Didn't he know she didn't care about words right now? Didn't he know she wanted him to kiss her?

"I said yes to the school dance... and to *Shaun of the Dead*," Kimmie said. "Now shut up and kiss me."

"Yes, ma'am," he whispered, and then brushed his lips across hers. His mouth felt warm and soft and gentle. She sighed when he moved away. His hand found hers, and they sat in silence. Hayden scooted closer and put his arm around her. Kim snuggled against his shoulder.

"So how do you know I wasn't asking to go steady with you?"

Kimmie looked up at him. "Go steady? What is this, the 1950s?"

"Go steady," he reiterated. "Girlfriend, boyfriend. Dates. Necking." He wagged his eyebrows, but she saw his nervousness.

She pretended to think about it. "I don't know..."

"Don't say anything yet," he interrupted. "Think about it. I can wait."

"Oh, Hayden." She laughed. "I've been waiting months for you to notice me. I'd like for us to be a couple."

"Wow," he said. "I've never not noticed you."

Kimmie felt his rapid heartbeat when she hugged him, her own heart bursting with joy.

Hayden leaned down and kissed her again.

"Wow," she said, echoing his earlier sentiment.

"Just wow." Happiness danced through her. Hayden was her boyfriend. She felt so...*weird*.

"So what were you crying about? Can I help?"

Misery crushed her joy. Hayden might have to wait until graduation to see her again once Mom figured out everything she'd done.

"We have a problem."

Kimmie and Hayden looked up. Tilda stood there, arms akimbo, her expression panicked. Jenny was right beside her, and she looked upset, too.

"What happened?" asked Kimmie.

"There's a disturbance in the force," said Jenny.

Hayden laughed. He stopped when he noticed the girls were not joining in. "You make a Star Wars joke, and I'm supposed to take that seriously?"

"I'll meet up with you later," said Kimmie, popping to her feet. She, Tilda, and Jenny hurried away, leaving behind a very confused boy.

SOMETHING WET AND ticklish licked her feet.

Natalie sat up, yanking her legs away from the offender.

She stared, and then yelled, "You!"

"Moo," said the ghost cow. *"Moooooo."*

CHAPTER TEN

MATT HEADED FOR the spot Natalie had pointed out earlier. She'd chosen a good place near the trees away from most of the crowd. He stepped around a game of horseshoes and increased his pace, eager to be alone with Natalie.

Then he heard the scream.

Natalie!

He sprinted forward, his eyes adjusting to the darkness. He saw three figures grappling. Natalie's white dress shimmered in the moonlight as she fought against her attackers.

Cold fear exploded in Matt's chest.

As soon as he got close enough, he skittered to a stop, his shoes sliding on the soft grass. Natalie looked helplessly at him while a badly dressed male ghost with a pencil-thin moustache and the spirit of an elderly woman in a jogging suit and orthopedic shoes struggled to hold on to her.

The persistent cow spirit lumbered in front of them and mooed.

Matt charged in, but the moment he tried to grab Natalie away from the ghostly trio, the spirits yelped as if he'd pinched them.

Everyone disappeared.

"Natalie!"

THE GIRLS SNUCK into Tilda's room, and shut and locked the door. Tilda sat on the bed, her eyes wide. "We're screwed. A demon came through the portal."

"Demon," said Kimmie, horrified. "Are you sure?"

"Yes," hissed Tilda. "I'm sure. I did a location spell, but got nada. But there's definitely an evil entity loose in the town." She pointed to an opened book. "Turns out the spell I used isn't that picky about what it draws in. Apparently, one of the reasons most witches don't use it is because demons and other nasty things sometimes ride piggyback on spirits."

"Ohmigawd! Why would you use a spell like that?"

"Well, it would've been fine," said Tilda, "if you hadn't broken the circle!"

"I didn't intend for Broken Heart to get overrun by ghosts and demons," yelled Kimmie. "I wanted vampires."

"You should've said that. How easy is it to say *vampires* instead of *dead guys*?"

Kimmie opened her mouth then snapped it shut. "You're right. I suck." She plopped down on the bed next Tilda.

"The binding spell will work for the ghosts, but

not the demon," said Tilda.

Jenny sat next to Kimmie and patted her back. "We have to tell the adults."

"We are so dead," said Tilda.

"Yeah." Kimmie sighed. "I'm gonna be grounded until I'm forty-two."

"Me, too," said Jenny. "Nice knowing y'all."

NATALIE POUNDED ON the door. She was locked inside her own basement, thanks to Kenny Rogers, his awful mother, and that goddamned cow.

What the hell was going on?

She screamed, hoping someone would hear her. But everyone was at the barbecue. They wouldn't know where to find her. And who would think to look for her at her own house?

"Hey! Let me outta here!"

The door swung open and Natalie stepped back, shocked when she recognized the man standing.

"Phil?"

"I am the Dark One." His beady brown eyes took in her dress, bare feet, and mussed hair. He frowned. "I thought you were dead."

"I am," she snapped, elbowing him out of the way. "Why aren't *you* dead?"

"You can't kill me. I'm the Dark One," he intoned.

"I'm getting the hell out of here," Natalie said, but not-so-dead-undead Phil grabbed her arm and swung her back into the room. "Hey!"

"Your husband heard the call about your love life and contacted me through spiritual means right away. He's been trying to get back into my good graces for a long while now."

"What is that supposed to mean? How did Ronald

get a call about my love life?"

"Ah, yes. Unfortunately, Ronald is no more. He died in the service of his dark lord." He bared his fangs, which were oddly long and knife-sharp. "Plus, he was delicious. Desperation adds a certain delectable flavor."

Natalie stepped back. "You ate him?" Appalled, not because Ronald was dead, but because, *ew*. Ronald was rotten, and she imagined his blood would taste as unpleasant as he was.

"You were his entrance fee into the group. When you disappeared, before I could drain you dry, I had to make an example of him. No take-backsies."

When she'd agreed to go on the blind date, Phil had shown up and driven her to the abandoned church off Fremont Street. She'd been terrified, especially when she saw the robed figures and her ex-husband waiting for her. Ron had been so enamored of Phil and his Children of the Night organization that he'd lost his damned mind. Or maybe Phil helped him lose it. What had made her blood run cold was how unaffected Ron was when Phil drug her into his lap and starting sucking her blood.

Asshole.

Natalie wasn't human anymore. She'd been spent three years as a vampire, and she realized she wasn't scared of Phil. She peered up at him. "Have you always had that bald spot?"

Phil's hand automatically touched the back of his head.

Natalie stood, frowning. "And have you always been this, this bony?" She poked a finger in his chest. "And your nose—it's so long."

She put her hands on hips and gave the vampire a

good once-over. "You're shorter than I remember," she added.

Phil stared at her as if she'd sprouted horns and a tail. His mouth opened and closed like a fish. Finally, he sent her a haughty, superior look. "You shouldn't speak to the Dark One like that."

"The Dark One shouldn't refer to himself in third person. Get real, Phil" Natalie said, rolling her eyes. " You're a supernatural joke. You know what they say about undead guys like you, right? If you have long fangs it means you have a small dick."

He blushed to the roots of his hair—or lack thereof. She found that interesting because technically vampires didn't really have the blood circulation to turn that red.

Natalie looked at the man before her. She felt nothing. Zip. No resentment. No self-pity. No remorse. No fear. Sometime during the past couple of days, everything had changed. The past was the past. She was dead, and she'd accepted that. The Dark One aka Phil the Pathetic had no hold over her.

"I'm leaving now," she said. She shoved him, but he grabbed her easily again and pushed her back into the room. "What's wrong with you? You can't kill me."

"It's not your blood I seek," he crooned. "It's your soul."

Natalie's mouth dropped open. "Are you serious?"

"Yes. I'm serious." He blinked rapidly as if he'd expected this encounter to be going very differently. "You think I'm bad? The Darkest Dark One is way meaner than I am. I owe him a soul, and it's gotta be yours."

"The Darkest Dark One?" Natalie laughed.

"That's ridiculous."

Phil looked around, and then whispered, "Don't make fun of DDO. He doesn't like that." His fingers dug into her arms. "We all have our debts," he said. "And I must pay mine."

"Oh, this sucks," said Natalie.

"Tell me about it." Phil cocked his fist and hit her as hard as he could. Pain exploded in her head right before the world went black.

"WE'LL ORGANIZE A search party," said Mayor Hewie, pounding Matt on the back. "I'll call the Little People. They won't like that our Goddess Sparklenose has been kidnapped."

Matt stared at the spot Natalie had been not five minutes before. How could ghosts just take her like that? And why had they acted like he'd caused them pain? He stuck his hands into his short's pockets. What the— Frowning, he took out the tiny silk bag.

He looked up and saw Kimmie. She and her two friends stood a couple of feet away. The kid looked like she was getting ready to cry. Oh, no. He had a bad feeling.

"What is this?" he asked.

Kimmie swallowed hard. "It's a juju bag."

The three witch sisters, Lenette, Dorica, and Nell, who ran the bed and breakfast, arrived. Lenette, the curvy redhead, held out her hand and asked Matt, "May I?"

He gave her the bag. She opened it, looked at the ingredients and looked at her teenage ward. "Why did you make a ghost repellant?"

Tilda stared at the ground. "We, uh … sorta did a dating spell and ghosts, um, responded."

"Dating spell," said Dorica flatly. The short brunette crossed her arms. "For who?"

All three girls immediately looked guilty. Then Kimmie said, "My mom."

Matt stared at her. "You three are the reason all those ghosts showed up?"

"I'm sorry." Kimmie flinched. "I wanted her to have a love life. She deserves it. My dad was a real douchebag to her."

Jessica and Patrick joined the group, and Jess said, "What's going on?"

"Our children have cast a spell, and now Natalie has been ghost-napped," said Lenette.

Jessica faced her daughter. "Really? First the zombie and now this?"

"Kimmie needed me," Jenny said. "I'm totally grounded, aren't I?"

"Yes," said Patrick. He clamped a hand around her neck. "Startin' now."

"I'll help with the search," said Jess. She kissed her husband. Then she eyed her daughter. "You're going to be so busy for the next couple of months, we should change your name to Cinderella."

"Chores?"

"Soooooo many chores."

"Let's go," said Patrick. He wrapped his arms around Jenny and disappeared in a sparkle of gold.

"What did we tell you about spellcasting, Tilda? You have to train. That's why you're here! To learn the proper way to be a witch." Nell, who was blonde and medium height, took the bag from Lenette and peered inside. "This is three times more powerful than it should be. You better tell us the whole story."

NATALIE WOKE UP strapped to a recliner. She was still in her basement, but apparently Phil had been busy re-arranging her bedroom to accommodate whatever madness was about to occur.

Candles were lit throughout the room. They cast shadows on the ceiling and walls, making what used to represent safety and comfort into something creepy and deranged.

She tried to shift in the chair, but the ropes kept her pinned.

"It's not regular rope," said Phil. "It has silver threads and was enchanted by an evil witch."

"Lovely. Kill a lot of vampires for the Darkest Dark One, do you?"

Phil shrugged.

"Nothing but a sheep," Natalie said. She felt the room grow cold. Three shapes wavered into full-bodied ghosts: Kenny Rogers, his crazy mom, and the butt-biting bovine.

"What's with the cow?" she asked.

"Oh, don't you recognize him? You created a child with the nincompoop."

"What?" Natalie said alarmed.

Phil waved a grand hand, his expression brighter now that he'd managed to ruffle her composure. "That's Ronald." He studied the creature for a moment. "I don't know why he's manifested as a cow. I think it might be because I made him feel like a piece of meat. I mean, he was my dinner, after all."

"You're sick."

"Moooo," said Ronald.

"At least I'm not a cow in the afterlife." Ronald mooed again. Phil sighed. "Okay, okay. We're almost ready."

Natalie eyed Kenny Rogers, who couldn't quite meet her gaze. "Why would you do this?"

"No woman makes my baby feel bad," snapped his mother. She patted his shoulder. "How could you not want him? Look at how adorable he is!"

"I had know when to walk away," Natalie deadpanned, "and know when to run."

"That's not funny!" Kenny Rogers stamped his foot.

"Now, look what you did," seethed his mother. She patted faster. "There, there."

Natalie was quickly moving from panic to hysteria. She shouted, "Cut the apron strings, Kenny!"

"Shut up," he whined.

"C'mon, you're delivering me to Phil—"

"The Dark One!"

"—*Phil* and his super evil boss for revenge?"

"Damn right," said the mother from hell. "And you deserve it. My baby is too good for the likes of you anyway. Harlot! I saw you in that minivan with that flesh sack of a psychic."

Natalie blushed.

Ronald mooed again.

Kenny had the audacity to look like the injured party.

Phil waved at the mother and son. "Go away."

"We had a deal," said the mother. "We help you, and we get to stay."

"Do whatever you want," said Phil. "Just do it somewhere else."

Kenny and his mother faded away. Phil rolled his eyes. "They are so going back to limbo."

"Not a big fan of keeping your promises, are you, Phil?"

"I'm called the Dark One. Sheesh. People shouldn't expect me to be a good person."

"You're an awful person."

Phil smiled. "Thank you."

Natalie stopped fighting against the ropes and sank into the recliner. She needed to think about how to get herself out of this situation.

"Mooooo!"

"Be gone, foul cow," said Phil. He wiggled his fingers, and Ronald disappeared with a quick flicker.

"Is he gone, gone?"

"Yeah. That mooing was getting on The Dark One's last nerve," said Phil. "I'm ready now." He looked at Natalie. "The Darkest Dark One is about to arrive."

Peachy.

CHAPTER ELEVEN

AFTER THE GIRLS confessed what they'd done and admitted a demon, or something of that ilk, was running around Broken Heart, Matt walked away to gather his composure. He leaned against a tree and tried to settle his roiling emotions.

The idea that Natalie was in danger tore him to pieces.

"Mr. Dennison?" Kimmie stared at him, her lower lip trembling. "You can save my mom, right?"

"I'm going to try."

She nodded. "I really did just want her to be happy."

"I get it. But Kimmie, it's not your responsibility to make sure she's happy. If your Mom wanted a love life, she would have gotten one on her own."

"She did get one," said the girl. Tears fell. "I didn't know she was seeing you. She never said anything."

Matt didn't think it was the time or the place to explain the marriage ruse. He'd deal with that later, after he'd found Natalie safe and sound.

Kimmie put a hand on his arm. "Everyone says you're a psychic. Is that true?"

"Yes," he said.

"Then you can find Mom."

Matt wanted to reassure the girl, but after Natalie had slammed her mental door in his psychic face the first time he'd probed her mind, he'd been locked out. "I'll do my best, Kimmie."

"Yeah. Okay."

"Kimmie." Dorica waved the girl over. "You and Tilda will stay at the house with me."

"I want to help search," said Kimmie.

Dorica shook her head. "A lot of people will be looking for your mother. The best thing you can do is come with me and wait it out."

Kimmie trudged to join Dorica and Tilda, and the three of them left.

"All right," said Braddock Hayes, Broken Heart's security chief. "We'll set up a parameter search. Matt, you start at her house. Jess, Lenette, Lorcan and Eva, you go downtown…"

Matt's thoughts drowned out Brady's firm voice. He imagined his life would be like without Natalie. Bleak. Empty. She brought light into his darkness. Made him laugh. Frustrated him. He wanted more than just to take her to bed. He wanted to take her into his heart. As if he hadn't already.

Please, he begged whatever gods were listening, *let me find her.*

"Okay, people, let's move it." Brady clapped his hands. "Keep your cell phones or your telepathy on and contact me if you find anything."

The crowd dispersed, and Matt hurried to the minivan. He would do as Brady asked and check Natalie's house, but he didn't think she would be there. What kind of kidnappers took their victim home?

"STOP IT!" YELLED Natalie. "Stop it now!"

"The Darkest Dark One will not be denied," cried Phil. "Relent to the ultimate power of hell!"

"That's so gross," said Natalie. "Ugh!"

TEXTS CAME IN to Matt's phone as everyone reported in. Natalie was not downtown, at the diner, graveyard, or the abandoned convenience store at the edge of town.

Matt pulled into Natalie's driveway and parked.

He felt a shift in the psychic plane, a wave of desperation that had his heart turning over his in chest. *Matt. Matt. Matt!*

Natalie?

He felt the door to her mind open fully as her relief washed over him. *I'm in the basement of my house. Stop that!* She screeched—the horrible sound echoing inside his head. Fury roared through him followed by panic and fear. They were hurting her!

He jumped out of the car with cell phone in hand and called Brady. "She's at her house. She's being tortured."

"Wait for back-up," yelled Brady. "You're human, Matt. You can get hurt."

"So be it," he said. "Then I'll get hurt." No way could he wait. Not while Natalie's life was in the balance.

Matt tossed the phone and tried the front door. It was unlocked. Luckily, Natalie's house was two-bedroom ranch, and it only took him seconds to discover the door to the basement.

He was running on pure adrenaline and fear for Natalie. He rushed down the stairs, only to be confronted by a balding, bony, badly dressed vampire. The man showed his fangs and hissed. Yeah? Well, Matt was one of the most powerful Vedere psychics living, and he wasn't going to let this loser hurt anyone ever again. Matt grabbed him by the shoulders, and said as he projected his thoughts, "You're being eaten by rats." He released the image into the man's mind, planting it so firmly that the vampire would never be free of it. Not unless Matt removed it.

"Ah!" cried the bony vamp. "Get off me! Get off me! You can't eat the Dark One! The Dark One is uneatable!"

He jumped away from Matt, beating on his arms, chest, and legs. He ran around the room. "Get off me! Stop eating me!"

"Stop licking me, you rat bastard demon!" Natalie shouted. "Matt!"

Matt crossed the candlelit room and grabbed the bastard kneeling at her feet. He yanked up the slimy red thing and smashed a fist into its pudgy face.

"Did he touch you? I'll kill him." Matt growled, shaking the thing dangling from his grip. Dangling? Matt looked again. The demon was maybe three feet tall with black eyes and tiny horns protruding from his head.

Black blood gushed from the demon's nose.

Gold sparkles started appearing at spots in the

room and within moments, Jessica, Eva, and Lorcan shimmered into view. Jessica magicked her Ruadan swords and swung them both in an arc. "That the asshole?"

"The Darkest Dark One," said Natalie, her head slumping in relief.

"You mean the smallest small one," Jessica said.

"Are you okay?" Matt asked, holding the creature away from his body.

"He wanted my soul," Natalie replied.

Jessica stepped forward and put the point of one of the swords at the demon's throat. "Who the hell are you?"

"Bebeesus," sniffled the creature.

The door at the top of the stairs busted open and several people bolted down into the basement. Brady had his .9mm ready to go and did a sweep of the room. He looked at the creature Matt held. "That the asshole?"

"Yeah."

"Could someone release me from the chair?" asked Natalie.

Three vampires rushed to help her.

A loud scream startled everyone as a vampire leapt from the shadows and fell to the floor, squirming. "Make them stop! Their tiny teeth are like razors!"

"Jesus H. Christ," said Jessica. "Who's he?"

"Oh, that's Phil." Finally freed from the ropes, Natalie stood up, walked to the vampire, and kicked him hard in the balls. "That's for being a dick."

"What's wrong with him?" asked Eva as she stared at the writhing vampire with wide eyes.

"I implanted the idea he was being eaten by rats," said Matt. He dropped the demon, and the tiny beast hit the ground like a stone and cowered at Matt's feet. But Matt didn't care. He stepped to Natalie and drew her into his embrace. He cupped her face, looking her over for any wounds or trauma. He checked every part of her body that didn't warrant more privacy. She was trembling, but not injured. The fear gelled into relief. He kissed her soundly, reassuring himself that Natalie was alive-ish and all right. "What did he do?"

"He sucked my toes."

"He what?"

"He sucked her toes," repeated Jessica. "Pervert."

Lorcan burst out laughing, and Eva hit him. "It's not funny. He could have... bit her or something. Demon saliva is poisonous, you know. Should we call a doctor?"

"I neeb a boctor," the demon formerly known as The Darkest Dark One whined. "He broke by bose."

"You don't get a doctor," said Jessica. "You get a one way ticket back to the hell you came from, so shut up."

"What's going on?" Mayor Hewie bellowed as he pounded down the stairs, followed by Bettie, Lenette, and Nell.

"He sucked her toes," said Eva gravely.

"He sucked her toes?" Hewie bent down and shook a chubby finger in the demon's face. "Look here, mister, I don't know where you're from, but round these parts toe-sucking is simply not allowed." Hewie cleared his throat. "Do you mind? You're bleeding on my shoe."

Matt held on tightly to Natalie. He wanted to laugh, but he didn't. His emotions were so tangled that he didn't think he'd ever get them unknotted.

"I'd like to wash my feet," Natalie said.

"He didn't bite you, did he? No bruises?"

"No."

Matt felt a touch and looked down at Eva and Jessica. "We'll take her to the bathroom," said Eva.

"C'mon, Natalie," added Jessica. "Let's get the demon drool off your feet."

He hugged Natalie and kissed her cheek. He watched her and her friends leave the basement, and then looked down at the demon he'd punched.

"What do we do with him?" asked Matt.

Brady pulled out his cell phone. "We call the demon whisperers," he said, pushing buttons, "Phoebe and Connor will take care of him."

NATALIE DIDN'T KNOW whether to laugh or cry. She'd been scared witless about the idea of a demon feasting on her—as Phil kept exclaiming. Instead, the demon had sucked on her toes and slobbered on her feet.

Yuck!

Natalie stepped in the bathtub and scrubbed her feet under the rush of water from the tap. When Natalie felt clean, she turned off the water. "That was so weird."

"And disgusting," said Jessica, giving Natalie the towel.

Natalie shivered as she patted her feet dry. "He had a forked tongue, and it felt like sandpaper."

"Well, it's over now," soothed Eva. "The demon will get sent back to hell, and the ghosts will go to limbo. Everything will fine before dawn."

"Thanks," said Natalie. Speaking of ghosts, Ronald was dead. She didn't care about him, but she wondered how she would tell Kimmie. Did she need to tell her daughter? The man had been dead to them for three years already, so what did it matter? She led the girls into her kitchen and poured everyone a glass of lemonade. They sat down at the kitchen table.

"Okay," said Jessica. "Give. Are you marrying Matt?"

Natalie shook her head. "He's human."

"He's awesome," said Jess. "You two fit together. I think you should go for it."

"And bind him to me for a hundred years? That doesn't seem fair."

"He should probably get a vote," said Jessica. "Shouldn't he, Eva?"

Eva raised her hands. "It's not our business." She looked at Natalie and smiled. "I wouldn't give up on being with Matt, especially if you love him."

"Mom!" Kimmie appeared in the doorway. She ran toward her mother, and Natalie stood up and hugged her daughter. Kimmie started crying and apologizing.

"What's going on, sweetheart?"

"It's a long story," said Dorica from the doorway. "You better sit down."

CHAPTER TWELVE

NATALIE HAD GROUNDED Kimmie until she was forty-two. Kimmie had taken the grounding and the ban of all electronics without a murmur of complaint. Even though her daughter had damn well created a serious problem for Natalie and other Broken Heart folks, she seemed genuinely sorry and upset.

At least the demon had been returned to the bowels of hell, and all ghosts, except Jerry, had been expelled from Broken Heart and sent into limbo. Natalie decided it best to let her daughter know that her father had died—but didn't include the news about him being the ghost cow. There was no point, and though Kimmie had long ago accepted that her father had abandoned them, Natalie could see she was still hurt by the knowledge of his death.

When the events of the night before had wound down, Matt had kissed her good night. Natalie could still feel his lips against hers. The conversation with Eva and Jessica about marrying Matt gave her hope that maybe she and the psychic could have something wonderful together one day. Maybe.

In the meantime, she'd been called to the Emporium by Bettie and her bridal squad. Natalie figured she might as well go and finally dispel the whole marriage myth.

As she closed the door behind her, she heard the cough of an engine. Turning, she caught sight of Mr. Smith, Bettie's husband, backing out his 1957 Ford.

"Natalie," he called out. "Get in. Bettie says I'm supposed to take you to the Emporium."

"Thanks," said Natalie. She slid into the car. "I have my own wheels, you know."

"Yep." Mr. Smith pulled out into the street and sped up to a whole ten miles an hour. "You and Matt will do just fine. Long, happy marriage like me and my Bettie. Me and the missus have been married two-thousand and thirty-three blessed years."

"That's wonderful," Natalie said, trying not to watch the speedometer. "But I don't think Matt and I are going to get hitched. Do you think you could go a bit faster?"

"Speed limit," Mr. Smith said. "No reason to get your knickers in a knot, young lady. We get there when we get there."

They crept into the parking lot at a snail's pace, and Natalie resisted the urge to jump out of the vehicle. Mr. Smith circled the lot three times before finding a suitable spot. Despite her impatience, Natalie waited for him to get out of the car, lock the door, put the keys in his pocket, and finally, *finally*, shuffle toward the Emporium's entrance.

When Natalie and Mr. Smith entered the building, people milled around smiling and laughing.

"There you are!" Bettie kissed her husband on the cheek, and then she latched onto Natalie's arm. "We have a surprise for you, dear."

Dread and resignation filled Natalie. She couldn't escape fate, at least not the fate engineered by the residents of Broken Heart. She followed Bettie reluctantly. Maybe she should just confess everything to Bettie right now. The whole town would learn of Natalie's deception within the hour and she could go home and drink vodka martinis.

Instead, she trailed Bettie through the building, down the hall, and into a large room. A huge banner proclaiming, "Congratulations Matt and Natalie" hung against the back wall. Every resident in Broken Heart appeared to have crowded into the room.

"Surprise! The whole town wanted to celebrate your happiness with you," Bettie said.

Hewie Twinkletoes stepped forward. "Seems like your wedding day got moved up, but the Little People and I sure do hope you'll still be at our ritual god and goddess on Saturday. You and Matt are the perfect Glimmerrod and Sparklenose." Hewie squeezed her shoulder, gave her a wide smile, and then meandered toward a table filled with food

"Hello, pretty mama," an Elvis-like voice intoned.

Bettie nodded at Natalie, and then took her husband over to the punch bowl.

"Getcha to the church on time?" Frank curled his lip in an Elvis sneer and tugged his purple cowboy hat. "Thank ya, thank ya very much."

"Okay then."

Frank nodded and wandered away.

Eva and Jessica found her and dragged her away to a corner.

"Holy crap," said Jess. "What the hell is going on?"

"I think Bettie is trying to marry me off to Matt. Like right *now*."

"And what do you two want to do?" asked Eva.

"I think … I think I love him. And I want him. But a hundred years!" Natalie shook her head. "I can't ask him to give up his life to be in mine."

"Look, we can formulate an escape," said Jessica. "Just say the word, and I'll get you the hell out of here."

"No, you won't." Bettie appeared and yanked Natalie along to a white lace table that held several dozen bottles of champagne. Matt stood there, a glass of bubbling liquid in his hand. Bettie shoved one into Natalie's grasp. "The groom's here! Time for a toast!"

Natalie stared at him, eyes wide. Then she remembered he could read her thoughts. *Are we going to let this continue?*

Yep.

What?

"Toasts to the happy couple," Bettie trilled. "Who's first?"

"May they love each other tender," came Frank's southern drawl. "And get all shook up in happiness."

People laughed and drank. Matt tapped his glass with hers and sipped. She did, too, trying not to choke on the pale, sweet liquid.

"May your love bloom and grow," said Mr. Smith. "And don't forget to prune those thorns!"

More laughing, tapping, drinking.

Several more toasts rang out, and Natalie felt worse and worse. For a moment, she imagined her and Matt were truly engaged, that all the well-wishing and cheers and teasing meant something. But reality intruded. She wasn't going to trap Matt into a hundred-year mating, no matter how much she wanted him, or how much she wanted this wedding to be real. She figured it was time to admit her mistake, face it, and live with it.

She had to stop this. Now.

"Everyone," Natalie spoke above the chattering. "I have something to say."

"Sshhh," Mrs. Smith said. "Natalie wants to toast the groom!"

I want to be with you. Matt's words in her mind startled her.

She turned to him and her breath caught. He was gorgeous. Funny. Sincere. He'd given her so much—more than he would ever know. She wished things were different … that they were two humans who could date, love, and yes, one day, marry.

His gaze caressed her face, and she didn't want to interpret the emotion in his eyes. It was too soft, too tender, too much like love, for her to tolerate. She turned and faced everyone, her heart breaking at all the smiles aimed her way.

"You've all been very kind," she said. "But I'm afraid there's been a huge misunderstanding." She took a deep breath.

"Natalie." Matt put down his champagne and drew her into his embrace. "I'm in love with you. Marry me. Say yes." He caressed her cheek with his thumb, and Natalie felt shock arrow through her.

"You'll die before I will."

"I'll die without you."

"No, you won't."

"Natalie." He kissed her softly. "I'm yours. So please, be mine. Say yes," he said again.

"What in the blue blazes is going on!" Bettie pointed at the two of them. "You two are in love, and that's a fact."

"You are," said her husband. "We'd know, too. We're romance fae."

"Like Cupid?"

Bettie rolled her eyes. "Do not get me started on Cupid. Like the Greeks cornered the market on love."

Mr. Smith patted his wife's arm. "Now, dear, let's not ruin their happy day."

"Thanks, everyone," said Matt. He pulled Natalie away from the table and swung her up into his arms.

"What are you doing?"

"You're being wishy-washy, so I'm taking you home," he said. "And then … I'm just gonna take you."

Hot and cold shivers invaded her. Making love with Matt. Binding with him. "Are you sure?"

"Damn right." Matt carried her outside and put her into his Jeep. "I'm psychic, Natalie. I know my own mind better than most. And my own heart. You and I are good together."

In no time at all, they were near Matt's house. The tires screeched as he pulled the car into his driveway and threw the gearshift into park. He leapt from the Jeep, ran around the passenger side and opened her door. He scooped her up once more.

Nerves tingling, they entered his home. Matt flicked a small lamp, which only illuminated the table on which it sat and part of the burgundy couch. Natalie closed the front door and leaned against it, uncertainty eating away at her.

"God, you look beautiful," Matt said. Natalie's head snapped up, and she drew in a breath at the stark desire reflected in Matt's eyes. She licked her dry lips and tried to speak, but the words caught in her throat.

"Stay there."

Matt disappeared into the bedroom. He reappeared seconds later, completely naked. His arousal jutted, beckoning her. Sharp desire ripped through her.

"Matt."

He surrounded her, putting his hands on either side of her face. Leaning down, he kissed her, his lips devouring hers. He cupped her breasts, pressing his erection against her. He pulled a scant inch away and looked at her, his eyes hungry, needy.

"Unless you have a preference," he whispered. "I thought I'd take you here first."

"T-take me?"

He unzipped the dress, sliding the straps off her arms. The material pooled at her feet. Then he wiggled off her underwear. "I've spent a lot of time thinking about you, Natalie. What happened in the van was incredible. But I want everything, and the waiting's killing me."

His words, accompanied by his hot, fervent touches, held her hostage. She wanted him. They had all night to explore each other, to take things slowly. To make sure that he really, really, *really* wanted to do this.

He bent to stroke her breasts with his tongue, and

she moaned. He lifted her, and she wrapped her legs around his waist. "Be sure," she whispered.

"I am," he said, positioning himself between her thighs.

"Yes," she said.

He paused and stared into her eyes. "Yes?"

"Yes," she said again. "I'm yours."

A smile curled Matt's lips. "About time." Slowly, he entered her wet heat and within seconds he'd filled her completely.

Natalie dotted kisses on his face and neck, rubbing her breasts on his chest. His hands grasped her hips, and she held onto his shoulders, urging him closer. Her pleasure expanded, encompassed.

"I want to bite you," she said. "I think I need to."

"Do it."

She sank her fangs into the side of his neck. His warm blood filled her mouth, and as she drank, his movements quickened.

"That feels incredible."

She tightened around him, drawing him in deeper. She licked the wound she'd created with her fangs, and then looked at Matt. His green eyes glittered fiercely, sending a feminine satisfaction thrilling through her. His mouth found the taunt peak of her breast. "Oh, Matt," she cried. The wondrous feeling swelled, crested, burst into a thousand sensations. "Matt!"

Even as she pulsed around him, he cried out, his own release throbbing inside her. He dropped his head to her shoulder, and kissed the hollow at the base of her throat.

"When I recover sufficiently," he muttered, "we'll go to the bedroom."

"Hurry up and recover."

He nipped her collarbone, then turned, held her around his waist and walked to the bedroom.

"You can let me go," Natalie said.

"No way. Never." He sat down on the bed, still inside her. His grin was sexy and wicked. "Shall we begin again?"

NATALIE SPRAWLED ON top of Matt, her cheek pressed against his heart. He stroked her back, smiling as she wiggled against his fingers and demanded, "Scratch, please."

He did, and she practically purred. "I like that."

She slid off and leaned on her elbow, looking at him. Matt turned on his side, facing her, gently stroking her hip. He hadn't been able to keep his hands off her since they'd started their lovemaking fest. He had to touch her. It was a Natalie Addiction.

Matt trailed a finger down her breast and encircled the hardening nipple. "I have strawberries and whip cream."

Her gaze brightened and she licked her lips. "Really?"

Two hours and one bottle of whipped cream later, Matt kissed the last of the strawberry juice from Natalie's lips.

"That was fantastic," she said. "What can you do with a cantaloupe?"

He chuckled. "I'm game to find out. How do you feel about a long, hot, steamy bath with a naked man?"

"Hell, yes."

He looked at her. A drop of red juice trailed down her neck, and he traced the wet line. A testament to her unfettered response to his lovemaking. He'd never felt so grateful before. He knew the gift Natalie had given him—even if she didn't.

Her gaze softened and she planted a kiss in the center of his chest. "Now about that bath...."

CLEAN AND DRY, Natalie snuggled against Matt. He pulled her closer, murmured her name, and then slipped back into sleep. She pulled the comforter over his chest, though it was a shame to cover any part of Matt.

The digital clock on the nightstand blinked three a.m. Okay. She'd let him have a nap.

MATT STIRRED, OPENING his eyes. His body, on full alert, vibrated with intense pleasure. His fists clenched the sheets as he realized what had awakened him.

Natalie.

She kneeled between his legs, head bent, her wicked mouth caressing him. As her tongue tasted his arousal, he jerked against her lips.

"Woman, are you trying to kill me?" His eyes adjusted to the darkness of the bedroom and he suddenly wished for light. He wanted to watch Natalie take him.

"No, just a wake up call." Her deep, throaty laugh was the laugh of a vixen. Fierce, aching need ravaged his body. Impatient, he tugged Natalie forward.

She needed no other coaxing. Her slick, warm flesh accepted him one tortuous inch at a time. Matt grasped her hips and entered her fully, groaning at the tight, velvety clench. Her tentative movements almost destroyed his willpower. He allowed her full control, even as her hesitant tests of his flesh drove him wild. Matt cupped her breasts, urging her close so that he could sample the taunt peaks. She moaned, placing her hands against his chest, her fingers digging into his skin. Her pace increased and Matt suckled one nipple, teasing and pulling.

Natalie's scent teased his nostrils, and her sounds of pleasure accented his own. He knew she was close, so close...he stilled her hips and flipped her over, withdrawing.

She cried out, her closed eyes flying open. "Matt!"

"Hang on, sweetheart," he murmured. He clicked on the small lamp near the bed and looked at Natalie. Her gorgeous hair spread over the pillow and her shoulders. He stroked her temple, smiling at her half-lidded gaze begging for him to finish the act she'd started. Then he looked at her lips, swollen from her earlier loving of him.

Both temptress and innocent.

He felt an emotion so tender, its very softness sliced him to the core. She was his woman now, and his alone, and he would not waste one minute. He kissed her, tasting himself on her lips. Raising above her, he watched her watch him. His emotions made him quake inside. He thought he'd known love before, but he hadn't. He'd never felt this way before about another person in his life. Ever.

"What is it?" she asked, tasting his skin. The flick of her tongue against his nipple made him shudder. Damn, she felt good.

Matt nipped her shoulder. She bucked against him, but he pulled back. She stared at him, frustration and need evident in her dark gaze.

He looked at her body, his gaze devouring every

perfect inch of her. He put his fingers against her neck, feathering her skin lightly. She trembled, and he knew she was experiencing the same ache claiming him. He stroked a slow line to her breast, encircled her nipple, and then touched her ribs, stomach, and hip. She moaned softly as his fingers trailed to her center. He hesitated and put his thumb against her core. Her gasp was sharp, insistent. She was wet, warm...ready.

She moved against his touch, and Matt thought about ending the whole game. He needed to feel her around him.

He couldn't explain the jolt of electricity echoing through him. He pressed his palm against her mound, dipping a finger into her.

Matt groaned and covered her, allowing his erection to slide against the nest of curls hiding her sensitive flesh. She adjusted her position, and Matt felt her hands on his buttocks, urging him to enter.

Her gaze was liquid, hot.

The fire, the need, roared through him.

Natalie pulled him close, and he plowed into her with one swift stroke, his orgasm so close, he had to stop. Natalie didn't, though, her hips rose and fell, taking him completely. She clutched his shoulders, wrapped her legs around his waist as she pushed upward. A long, low moan escaped, then she pulsated around him, her woman's rhythm shattering his tenuous control. Matt exploded, thrusting deeply, Natalie's name escaping his lips as he tumbled over oblivion's edge.

NEAR MORNING, THEY'D finally left the bedroom for the kitchen. "What is this?" Natalie asked as Matt put the loaded plate on the table.

Food hunger had temporarily overcome other appetites. Natalie looked at the microwave's clock. Five a.m. Her time with Matt was ending too quickly.

"I need to go home," she said. "Dawn will be here soon."

"Stay here," he said. "I'll watch over you."

Natalie inhaled, smelling the rich scents of eggs, bacon, sausage, and biscuits. She grinned at him. "This is your idea of breakfast?"

"It's my Heart Attack on a Plate special. Dig in." He poured coffee and gave her a wolfish grin. "You look too tempting in my shirt. I'm not done ravishing you."

Her fork clattered to the table. "I'm finished. Besides those shorts have to go. I prefer you naked."

"Thank God," he murmured. Then he wagged his eyebrows. "You need food to keep up your energy level."

"You mean you do. My energy level's fine," she said, but picked up the fork and began to eat. The food was wonderful, but more wonderful still was Matt's preparation of it. It seemed like such a husbandly thing to do.

"I need to tell you something."

Natalie put her fork down and folded her hands. She suspected Matt did not share much about his life with others. He looked like a vulnerable little boy, beseeching her forgiveness.

"You know I used to be a Vedere psychic. I was engaged to another Vedere, a woman named Vera."

"Vera Vedere?"

He laughed. "No. Vera Williams."

"The Vederes are close knit. Some factions are

arrogant and feel superior. Vera came from one of those. She was power hungry. I didn't know it at the time, but she's willing to do anything to climb to the top of Vedere ruling council. Including marry a man she didn't love."

Natalie felt a rush of sympathy coupled with anger. How could anyone who knew Matt for two seconds not love him? "I'm sorry." She reached across the table and squeezed his hand.

"I found her in bed with another councilman. And then I began to understand that was only the first of her betrayals. The Vederes are not to be trusted," he said. "Taking myself out of their game put a dent into their political scrambles. I thought I loved Vera, but Natalie … what I felt for that woman isn't even one-tenth of how I feel about you."

"I love you, too."

Matt gestured around them. "We can change anything in this house. We'll redo it however you want. Or we can live in your house. Or we can buy a new one. Whatever you want, Natalie. Talk it over with Kimmie. This will affect her to. I just want you happy. I'll do whatever it takes to make you happy."

She loved that he thought about her daughter, taking her kid's well-being into consideration. "You make me happy." She went to him and sat on his lap.

His eyes darkened with desire. Matt trailed her ribcage slowly, settling against her hips. Warm strokes over her hips, down her thighs, then under the shirt, until his hands rested on her waist.

She wrapped her arms around his neck and kissed him. Matt's fingers slipped downward and stilled. He broke the kiss, looking down at her in shock.

"I must have forgotten to put on panties."

He swung her into his arms again and stalked out of the kitchen.

"Where are we going?" she asked even as they entered the bedroom. Matt laid her on the unmade bed and crawled next to her.

His wicked grin sent hot sparks dancing through her.

CHAPTER THIRTEEN

"YOU MAY KISS the bride," Frank a.k.a. Elvis intoned.

Matt lifted Natalie's purple veil and kissed her soundly. Cheers, whistles and clapping erupted in the stone circle. The muggy heat of another Oklahoma night didn't bother Natalie at all. "I love you," she whispered against his lips.

"You better," he answered. "You're mine forever."

The Little People danced around. "Our god and goddess have mated," they shouted. "Fertility is ours!"

They threw pebbles at the happy couple.

"Ow!" said Matt.

"Now, now," said Hewie, wading through the paranormals that were knee-high to him. "That's enough pelting." He dotted his eyes with a handkerchief. "That was best Glimmerrod and Sparklenose ceremony I've ever seen. Elvis was a nice touch."

"Oh dear," Bettie said, sobbing. "It was so beautiful when he sang 'Love Me Tender'."

Bettie hugged them both. Others came forward offering best wishes and congratulations and knowing grins. Matt accepted hugs and kisses, keeping his arm tight around Natalie.

Jessica and Eva bestowed kisses and whispered sex advice, and made Natalie laugh.

"Mom!"

Matt and Natalie turned and saw Kimmie, Hayden, Tilda and Jenny standing nearby.

Kimmie hugged Natalie, then Matt. Joyous tears glittered in her eyes. "You're happy, Mom. I'm happy. We are so..."

"Happy," Jenny said sardonically.

"Elvis has the Cadillac ready. Go start your honeymoon!"

Matt grabbed Natalie's hand. "That's best idea I've heard all day."

Her brows rose. "Oh really?"

"Second best," he amended quickly, then pulled her into his embrace and kissed her breathless.

"Wait," Natalie said.

Matt raised a question brow. "For what?"

Natalie nodded to Kimmie, and her daughter carried over a perfectly, golden brown, deep-dish apple pie. Natalie grinned at the befuddled expression on Matt's face. "I promised you pie."

"You certainly did," he said.

He kissed her hard with a fervor Natalie would definitely explore later. When he broke from the kiss,

Natalie hadn't realized Kimmie had moved in so close to them, and her elbow whacked her daughter's arm, sending the pie catapulting into the air. It finally landed in a heap next to a crowd of Little People, who screamed and ran away.

"Oops," said Natalie.

Matt laughed and then swooped his bride downward, kissing her silly.

They left the stone circle and walked through the field toward the pink Caddy. Trailed by well-wishers, birdseed flew skyward, and scattered across the ground and the Caddy.

Matt tucked his bride inside the car, then rounded the trunk, getting into the other side.

"Ready?" he asked.

"Oh, yeah," said Natalie. "Ready."

LYCAN ON THE EDGE
SNEAK PEEK

SOPHIE LENNOX STARED at the watery muck because she had always faced reality head-on ... and, well, she had no other choice. She'd rather stare at the ground, anyway, because the other option was to stare at her breasts as gravity slowly squeezed them out of her pink bikini top.

If only she could shift. But going werewolf now would only complicate the already complicated mess.

At least hanging upside down from the seven foot Ladder of Doom had certain advantages. Since all the blood had rushed to her head, she no longer felt the pain in her rope-entangled feet. She sighed. The low breath skimmed down her heated face; she got a whiff of the faded mint smell of her toothpaste. Oh good. At least she'd have decent breath when she expired from the heat...if she didn't die of embarrassment first.

Painting her grandmother's shutters "Gingerbread Pink" should have been easy. When she tied the ropes around the paint cans and looped them over the ladder's tray, she raised and lowered the heavy cans several times. Then she climbed up, putting her weight on the step with the printed warning "Do Not Stand On This." The ladder wiggled. She wiggled. She fell backwards. The ropes wrapped around her ankles, suspending her above The Hole.

Attempts to reach up and disentangle her feet had been useless. Help was nowhere near thanks to the location of the decrepit old house. In Broken Heart, no one could hear you scream.

Ha, ha.

Well, no one in the vampire seniors nudist colony, which was just up the road. Come to think of it, she would prefer not to be rescued by the wrinkly, naked undead. Where the heck was her grandmother? How long did it take to pick up a few groceries? Sophie groaned. She'd been trapped on this stupid ladder for...

Aeons.

Hours.

She turned her wrist over and read the upside-down digital display. Oh.

Five minutes.

Her left breast shifted, threatening to expose its nipple. She tucked it in, wondering if she dared to untie and re-tie her bathing suit top. It needed to be tightened if she hoped to keep her breasts covered. Her gaze flitted around the side yard. The six-foot-tall fence a few feet away separated Gran's home from the nextdoor neighbor's. The bushes beside the ladder concealed most of her and, since they loved on the road to nowhere, she had o fear being seen by passing motorists. Or werewolves.

Wouldn't her friends just die? They would never let her forget.

Goddess, please kill me.

The right breast crept toward freedom.

Frustration shot through her. "All right. That's it!"

Damned if she was going to die suspended upside-down from a ladder with her breasts dangling from her bikini top like discarded Christmas-tree ornaments. Sophie reached behind her back and fumbled with the string. All she had to do was tighten it. Maybe she could just pull the loops—

The string loosened and released. The top swung off and dangled from her neck.

A string of curses erupted from her as she grabbed the top and pushed it against her uncooperative bosom. She couldn't get her boobs into position *and* re-tie the top. She pressed the material and her arms against her chest and closed her eyes in despair.

"Werewolf yoga?"

The deep, masculine voice startled Sophie. Her eyes flew open and she found herself staring at a jean-clad crotch. She closed her eyes, and opened them. The bulge was still there. It was rather large, she noticed.

What the hell was she thinking?

She tried to wriggle away, but swayed forward, bumping into *it.*

The man jumped back, missing the water-filled hole by scant inches. Mortification scorched her cheeks. *I'm half-naked, upside down, and now I've informally met a stranger's genitals.*

The jeans moved forward. Her gaze riveted to the steel buttons glinting in the morning sunshine. Irrational panic consumed her.

The crotch was returning.

Sophie screamed. The man retreated. He hunkered down, his expression one of concern. "Are you okay?" he asked, his voice gentle.

She swallowed her embarrassment, feeling foolish. "I'm fine. Who the hell are you?"

"I'm Daniel. You must be Sophie."

"How do you know that?"

"Because I met Virginia yesterday. She offered me the garage apartment in exchange for helping fix up the house."

Her grandmother hired some random werewolf dude to help with repairs? *What am I? Chopped liver?* She could smell his otherness. Daniel was definitely a werewolf. But she'd never seen him before. And in Broken Heart, everyone knew everyone.

He frowned. No, smiled. Sophie bent her neck, getting a sideways view of his face instead of an upside-down one. He was too young to be a neighbor and too handsome to be a comfort. He'd done nothing threatening. It wasn't his fault, his, er, bulge was eye level to her or that she was bumbling idiot. Sweat dripped from her brow as her body protested its unnatural position. Her arms had lost sensation, and her breasts were about to introduce themselves.

"Thanks for offering to help, but I'll just wait for my grandmother."

"I'm not leaving you here like this. You look like you're in pain and the ropes haven't been too kind to your ankles. They're bleeding."

"Oh." She swallowed heavily. "My bikini top, uh, came loose."

"I see."

"You do? Oh my God!" She looked at her chest, but her arms still provided sufficient cover.

"No, no. I don't see your—I can't see anything. I meant I understood." He looked away, and then returned his gaze to hers. His eyes were dark brown, reminding her of her favorite chocolate truffles. They held an indecipherable emotion in check. She suspected he found some humor in the situation and she felt grateful he hadn't laughed. "Do you want me to help you tie your bathing suit top?"

Her expression must have revealed her answer because before she could blurt out *Hell no!*, he stood and took off his white T-shirt. He squatted again then pushed the shirt over her head, gently tugging her ponytail through. "Do you think you can get your arms through it?"

She nodded.

"I'll go away and you holler when you're ready."

Sophie waited for him disappear around the corner of the house. She hurriedly put on the shirt and tugged the end over her stomach. Her arms felt achy and tingly, but she held onto the bottom seam for dear life. "Okay!"

He jogged back to her and grabbed the end of the shirt. "I'll tie it in a knot. It should hold until I get you untangled." His hands covered hers and suddenly the cold tingles pricking her fingers heated. "Your arms must feel like they're going to fall out of their sockets."

She nodded and reluctantly let go of the shirt. As he tied a tight, efficient knot, his knuckles brushed her abdomen. Her muscles tensed. When he stepped back to survey the ladder, she released a breath she hadn't known she'd been holding.

Daniel shook his head. "How did you manage to get the ladder between the holly bushes," he pointed to the puddle, "this swamp and the house?"

"I'm very talented," she grumbled. "Do what you have to, but do it quickly because I can't feel my feet anymore."

"Wrap your arms around me and hang on so you won't fall when I get you loose. I'll hold onto your legs and lower you to the ground."

Humiliation flooded her as the man stood and reached for her feet. Her breasts pressed against his flat stomach as she tucked her face between his legs. She hugged his muscular thighs and tried not think about the man's anatomy, in particular, the part located under her chin.

Sophie felt his grip around her knees as he tugged on the ropes. Then she felt a warm palm sliding between her thighs.

The ropes loosened, and her knees connected with his shoulders as her feet were freed. He tilted, his sneakered feet scrambling for purchase on the wet grass. His grip on her legs tightened and Sophie had no choice but to hold on for dear life as they both tumbled into the puddle.

Sophie spluttered as gritty water showered her face and filled her mouth. Since she'd landed on top, she had the advantage. She quickly turned around and plunked herself squarely on the man's chest with enough force to expel whatever air he had left in his lungs—which couldn't be much considering how hard he'd smacked into the ground. Mud and grass covered his face and hair and most of his clothes. A pair of brown eyes blinked at her as he tried to draw in a breath.

Sophie put her hand against his throat, pressing against his windpipe.

"I surrender," he gasped out, holding up his hands.

"What are you doing here?"

"Rescuing a crazy-assed werewolf." Then he grinned, his teeth flashing white through his muddied features. His stomach muscles flexed under her rear end and Sophie realized he was *allowing* her to sit on his chest and bully him.

The realization came too late. Before Sophie could scramble off, he grabbed her wrists and flipped her onto her back. Her werewolf surfaced and began to growl.

"Whoa, now." His eyes held a teasing glint, and his body was relaxed, not rigid with tension or intent to harm. What an odd thing to realize about a serial killer, she thought dazedly. She probably had a concussion.

Sophie considered her options. She could knee him, she supposed. She flexed her fingers, noting that his hands lightly held her wrists.

For a long moment they stared at each other, panting heavily. A woodsy scent—his cologne—filtered into her senses. She heard the buzz of bees around the honeysuckle bushes, the start of a lawnmower, the rapid beating of her own heart.

"Sophie!" Gran's voice trilled. "I see you've met Daniel."

The man rolled off Sophie. She balanced on her elbows and stared at her grandmother.

Gran smiled down as if Sophie and Daniel weren't

covered in mud. "Daniel, er, Mr. Clayton is my new handyman. He's going to help us with the house."

"You could've told me yesterday," accused Sophie.

"I forgot, dear. I'm old." Gran's gaze transferred from Sophie's mud-spattered clothes to the ladder. "What were you doing?"

"Painting the shutters," answered Sophie. She glanced at Daniel, who was trying to wipe the mud off his face and chest. The curly brown hair on his chest narrowed down his washboard stomach, the silky line of hair disappearing into the jeans. Tan, muscled, and good-looking. She looked at her grandmother and frowned. Suspicion crept through Sophie like a cautious spider.

"Where did you find Daniel?"

"Damian recommended him."

"You consulted with the king of werewolves about a handyman?" Sophie eyed Daniel, who shrugged. "Seriously?"

Gran tsked tsked, then made shooing motions at Sophie. "Go take a shower, Sophie. Daniel, you need one, too. Go on, now, both of you!"

"Virginia! Are you suggesting I shower with this woman?"

"Daniel, you devil!" Gran slapped her thigh and hooted.

Sophie whirled around.

Daniel's mouth quirked up at the corners, amusement dancing in his brown eyes. He shrugged. "If it means keeping my job, I'll suffer through it," he said sadly.

Sophie fumed at the pitiful look he sent her. It was laced with just enough lasciviousness to make her want to poke out his eyes.

"Of course, you won't be shower-sharing with my granddaughter. It's not proper." Gran winked at Sophie. "Fun, but definitely not proper."

Sophie escaped to the back of the house. She trudged up the three steps and opened the screen door. She plopped down on the floor of the enclosed porch and began to take off her dirty socks and shoes. She managed to get her left foot free, but the right shoe had a lace full of knots.

Something about Daniel Clayton bothered her. He was too...handsome, she decided. And he had an irritating dimple near the right corner of his mouth.

Until recently, Sophie believed people had good intentions. She believed in giving everyone the benefit of a doubt and second chances, but after … well, *after*, she'd re-evaluated her position on positive thinking.

Positivity could get you killed.

The door screeched and Sophie looked up. Daniel entered, his muscled torso gleaming with sweat and dirt. She tore her gaze from the view and concentrated on the knot in the tennis shoe strings.

"Need help?"

Startled, Sophie dropped the strings. "No thanks."

He tilted his head. "I'm sorry I saw your panties."

"You saw my—oh, crap," she said, again gripping her slimy shoe strings, "I don't want to discuss my underwear."

"Red's my favorite color."

Sophie pretended not to hear him.

"I saw the scar on your back, too."

Sophie stilled. She didn't like talking about the scar with anyone—not even Gran. She blew out a breath. "I'd rather talk about my amazing red panties."

"I recognize that kind of wound," he said gently.

"Where did the Alberich find you?"

"Who says they did?"

"Your scar."

Fuck this. She used werewolf strength to shred the stubborn lace and whipped off her shoe and sock. She dumped them into a pile, and stood up. "Don't plan on sticking around," she said. "We don't need your help."

Sophie whirled around, bare feet prickled by the uneven floor, heading toward the door that led into the house. And away from Daniel.

"Sophie."

Her hand clenched the old metal handle. She looked over her shoulder. "What?"

"I have one, too," he said. He turned around and for the first time, she noticed the long thick scar flared at both ends.

She'd never met anyone else who'd survived an Alberich attack. The ancient hunters were thought to be extinct—and no longer a threat to werewolves. But a new order had arisen, and its ranks had started tracking werewolves.

And killing them.

Daniel turned back around, his gaze sympathetic. "We're lucky."

Sophie shook her head. "Not all of us."

Tears threatening, she hurried into the house—trying to run from the emotions churned up by Daniel, and the past that never seemed too far behind.

THE BROKEN HEART SERIES

ABOUT THE AUTHOR

Michele Bardsley is a New York Times and USA Today bestselling author of paranormal romance. When she's not writing sexy tales of otherworldly love, she watches "Supernatural," consumes chocolate, crochets hats, reads books, and spends time with her husband and their fur babies.

44315282R00084

Made in the USA
San Bernardino, CA
12 January 2017